Gret's Rock

Margaret O'Donnell

Through Life's Greatest Joys and Worst Fears, We Find Our Way Home

ISBN Hardcover: # 978-1-7370027-2-7
ISBN Paperback: # 978-1-7370027-1-0
ISBN Electronic: # 978-1-7370027-0-3
Library of Congress Control Number: # 2022918294

Edited by Kristin Davis
Cover design by Demetra Georgiou
Publishing Consultant PRESStinely, PRESStinely.com

Portions of this book are works of fiction. Any references to historical events, real people, or real places are used fictitiously. Other names, characters, places and events are products of the author's imagination, and any resemblance to actual events or places or persons, living or dead, is entirely coincidental.

Printed in the United States of America.

Margaret O'Donnell
GretsRock.com

MARGARET
O'DONNELL

Dedication

To my husband, Rick, my best friend.
The true "Rock" of our family whose strength continues to
amaze me everyday.

I Love You

Contents

Prologue

"Get Outside and Move, No Quit!"

The saying, "No Quit," that I learned in a support group became our family mantra. And it will always be our mantra. It resonated with me when I first heard it, and when I shared it with Rick he felt the same. We knew we would never quit on one another. We are a team for life, no matter what.

Another mantra became "GET OUTSIDE AND MOVE!" This one we learned from Rick's trainer. It, too, resonated with us. Working with physical therapy Rick learned inner strength, perseverance, and resilience. His trainer brought out a competitive drive and attitude that sparked Rick. It was his trainer who inspired Rick to work toward those goals and still works with Rick on those goals.

Looking back, I realize each therapist who worked with Rick was amazing. There were those who treated Rick at the hospital and trauma unit and those who helped him sit for the first time. There was the team at rehab who worked with Rick to regain functioning and the ability to come home. There was the team at rehab who pushed him to his limits and beyond, for a year, never giving up hope. There were many tears, laughter, and frustrations along the path. Not once did Rick complain. He knew what had to be done if he wanted his life back.

Rick's trainer was a rock for Rick. Never taking no for an answer. Pushing him and giving him confidence. He was a friend and a true athlete. He understood Rick and knew exactly what was needed to get him motivated.

I watched Rick push through every therapy and training session with such hope; knowing he would do it! There was much grief and sadness, and always hope! I knew he would never quit on himself or his family!

TIME CONTINUES TO CHANGE

Days turned into weeks and weeks into months and before I knew it Rick's accident was three years ago. It was as if time had stopped for us. We were in constant healing mode as the world continued to move forward. My kids went on with their lives, friends and family went on with theirs. But Rick and I stayed focused on his healing and having life come back stronger and stronger. There was not one day, one minute, one hour that we stopped working or stopped hoping. We never stopped believing this could turn out differently. We were so determined and so committed to the love we shared that no way in hell was our beautiful life going to be taken from us.

Sure, days are quieter now and conversations light, vacations look different, but one thing is constant, LOVE. Rick continues to work hard, and I am by his side. We will never give up on each other. Marriage is hard enough, never mind throwing in a Traumatic Brian Injury. What saved our marriage was my fight to take care of myself, Rick's fight to take care of himself, and our fight to take care of each other.

It's okay not to be okay, to not be perfect, to scream and to cry, and to be mad as hell. But how you respond to life is up to you. Go out and fight; fight for what you want and never give up hope. As caregivers, always take care of your needs first. Always ask for help. Don't wait… people want to help you. Take breaks for yourself. Find joys in your life, no matter how small or big. Taking care of yourself will help those you love to move on and heal.

After being the caregiver and in a survival role for so long, it's natural to feel lost and left out. Even completely overlooked and invisible. All the attention is on the loved one who is injured or sick. What do you do and how do you heal from this? Simply find your truth. Find what lights you up. Surround yourself with JOY and LOVE. Be kind to yourself, be patient, and know you are doing what you need to do. Never feel bad or guilty. Always take breaks. It is important to feel steady and rock solid; stay calm in the storms and always have a big, open heart.

When in Florida, I found I needed to remain steady, continue my meditation practice, and be at peace with what we had. True, the life we had was GONE, the relationships are different, conversations are different, where we go and how we navigate each and every day is now calculated and different, but the truth is, I am not different; I am actually myself again, my true authentic self. Growing stronger each day to take care of myself and my family. To navigate life independently and with confidence again. Sitting quietly, I was able to find JOY again and was able to accept what had happened. I felt the anger and hurt, and then let go of them.

I hope that by reading this book you will learn how to do the same with the anger, hurt, and pain in your life. I hope you will realize how important self-care is for all of us. Without it, there is no joy, love, or returning to life.

Chapter 1

What Happened?

"Look, Rick, this view is amazing," Peg said as she viewed the entire Burlington skyline with tears streaming down her face. Rick barely noticed or cared. She wanted so badly for him to walk up behind her and hold her tight, as if to never let go. But that would not happen for a very long time. She had always wanted to live in a city and now, not by choice, this would be her view for the next several months.

Seasons

Peg and Rick lived in a beautiful home in the small town of Williamston. The town was made up of a small main street with a bank, church, village store, and a beautiful private school where their two children were educated. The school sat in the middle of the town with a stone wall surrounding the campus. Each stone represented an alumni dating to the 1930's. The athletic fields were where Peg and Rick watched lacrosse and field hockey games each week. The fields spread out through the campus and students would practice and play sporting events daily. There was a chapel at the center of the campus and each week students would gather in the chapel for a school assembly.

Williamston was nestled among mountains and every season was a beautiful time of year. In fall, the colors were vibrant, the air was chilly, and the town looked like a painting. Winters were crisp and white, and the mountains were covered with blankets of snow. Looking out the kitchen window in winter gave Peg the feeling of being in a snow globe. The snow fell and did not stop until spring. The mountains were covered in white, with pops of color from the houses. Spring was green with flowers bursting everywhere. Summer was warm and bright.

Peg remembers the view of the mountain and is grateful for each change of season. Fall reminded her that school days would soon begin which meant busy days with homework and sports practices for their kids. Winter was a reminder that colder and shorter days were ahead, hockey practice for her son was beginning, and snowstorms would soon bring the kids in the neighborhood to her hill for sledding and hot cocoa.

With the warmer air of spring came walks outside and a reminder that summer would soon arrive. With summer's arrival they would leave for Pointe Verde to live by the sea.

She would pack the van on the last day of school, wait for the kids to get off the bus, and right into the car they went. They would meet Rick there as he would commute to and from work. They would hit the turnpike singing, laughing, and anticipating the summer months. The kids would jump out of the car when they arrived, take off their shoes, and not put them on again until September. Barefoot, flip flops, and sand all summer long.

Williamston was home, a community that came together in good times and bad. Women's groups that did much to support local charities and fundraising events. A strong church community and a strong school system where her kids made wonderful friends. It was a small town where most everyone knew one another, and everyone supported each other. She never realized how much she would miss this sense of community in the year ahead.

Peg's days in Williamston were simple. After saying goodbye to Rick as he left for his long commute to work in Port St. Louis, she would get their kids settled in school and move about her day. Volunteering was a big part of her life, both at school and in town. When Peg first moved to Williamston, she went to a meeting not knowing what to expect. She soon realized the women in the group were exactly who she wanted to surround herself with: humble, trusting women who cared about the good of the community and who lifted one another up at every opportunity. These women wrapped their arms around each other in times of crisis. Peg learned this firsthand when she had to reach out to them for support. Not missing a beat, these women would jump in and do what was needed, such as delivering meals to Peg's mother when Peg could not be there.

In addition to volunteering with the women's group, Peg taught yoga, which she loved! The training was a life changing eight months. Peg would leave Williamston every month for a long weekend of training and self-discovery, staying at their seaside home during this time. She would walk on the beach each morning and take in the cold air. The ocean was so different in winter. It was so quiet. The beach was empty of people, and she was surrounded by nature. The water was frozen; in the winter everything on Pointe Verde was white and brown. She would walk and welcome this change. It was a healing eight months, a time to be completely alone with herself, her thoughts, and her fears. A time to connect inwardly with herself. She learned what was holding her back from being her true self, and how to be strong. And how to show up as a YES and face fears head on, something she had never been able to do. She found her voice to not only teach, but to speak from her heart and truth.

The yoga studio in Williamston, where Peg taught, was home; a safe place for her and a place for her students to open up and let go of their worries. The studio was a calming space. It was simply beautiful due to its calming energy. The minute one stepped through the doors, the scent of white sage tickled the nose as it drifted through the hallways leading to the yoga room. The walls were soft yellow, plants were everywhere, and there was always a hug from whomever was there. These people became her "Yoga Bar Family." They offered support that was true and deep.

"It's okay…everything is exactly as it was supposed to be in the moment!" This is what Peg preached in every yoga class she taught. Live breath by breath; make each day count; do something special or significant in the day; take time to meditate; walk outdoors; be thankful for each blessing; keep a journal and write down three things you are grateful for each day—that is what she had been telling people and doing for the past six years.

When Peg signed up for her yoga teacher training, she had no idea how much it would help her in the future. It was life changing for Peg, as the next year would be—for different reasons.

When Peg first moved to Williamston and her beautiful neighborhood, Jill was just her neighbor. But she soon became a dear friend for life. Jill was an anchor in Peg's life. Guiding her as a big sister would, encouraging her to step out of her comfort zone and try new adventures. Peg fondly remembers standing in the driveway the day they moved in. Jill came over with her eleven-year-old daughter, Becky. Jill's warm greeting helped Peg realize they had made the right choice in building their home there.

Jill and Peg spent hours at an Italian coffee shop which reminded Peg of her dad every time she entered the store. The smell of the most delicious coffees brewing, out of this world egg sandwiches, salads, and the sounds of Italian music in the background were so comforting. It was a small shop with a few tables where people from town gathered to regroup. There was no rushing. Each order was done slowly and one at a time—making the food even more delicious. They sat for hours; talking, sometimes crying, and sometimes laughing. Secrets shared, inner most thoughts expressed. Fears talked about and belly laughing to the core.

When they moved to Williamston, Peg had been so sad to leave Henrietta and sobbed all the way down the turnpike. But the twenty years spent building their family in Williamston were the best years of their lives. The memories would forever be embedded in her heart. Rick, however, would not remember most of this time. In fact, most of their life would not be remembered, and they would soon be starting over.

Saying Goodbye

As Peg packed up the home and the memories they had shared for twenty years, it was all so bittersweet. Where to begin? Peg was one to save everything, not letting anything go. In the cedar closet there were boxes upon boxes of stored memories. Boxes of clothes her kids wore as babies. Clothes her parents bought for them. She remembers crying as she donated items and said goodbye to most of their things—just things she would remind herself months later.

The arrival of spring was a reminder that their lives were about to change forever. Their son, Peter, would be graduating high school in May. Shortly after graduation the car would be packed for their final trip down the turnpike to begin the life they dreamed of on Pointe Verde. They had always loved their summers spent at the seaside, and Rick and Peg had decided they would now make it their permanent home. They would be empty nesters after all, and they didn't need all the space and yard the Williamston house provided.

Their home of twenty years was packed and ready for sale. They were about to begin again…getting rid of the old and starting a new adventure. Rick always said to her, "It's about what is right for the four of us. The kids are away, why not try something completely new?" It was scary and exciting at the same time. Trusting that her husband always knew what was good for them and with optimism that everything would be okay, she went for it!

She walked through each empty room, saying goodbye to this life. Looking at the marks on the walls where photos had hung for so many years. Walking into the kid's rooms, remembering them as babies. She walked into her own bedroom and stood in the empty space where she had shared so much with Rick. Love making, deep secrets, and the grand plans they had made together.

The house was empty when they left and there was no turning back. And, so, there they were, driving on May 31st to Pointe Verde. The drive seemed longer than usual, maybe because it was the last time they would make the drive. She would never again spend a night in Williamston, that small New England town she would always call home.

Chapter 2

POINTE VERDE

Rick grew up summering on Pointe Verde in a small neighborhood by a beautiful river, and he wanted that for his own family. It was a neighborhood nestled around the river. Twenty years ago, Rick and Peg decided to buy a home on Pointe Verde in order to give that same experience to their children. When Rick took Peg to see the house, she was shocked. It was falling apart, and she could not see the possibilities of how to make it a home. But, as usual, Rick always saw the good, and she trusted him. So they bought the house! They bought the home and renovated it from top to bottom. Little by little, one brick at a time, they made it their home on Pointe Verde.

"Gret's Rock," as they came to call their home, was a small Pointe Verde cottage. Three tiny bedrooms, a small living room, and a kitchen. This small house brought joy and love to their days. Beach days and sunsets and beautiful memories to last a lifetime. There was always sand on the floor and dishes in the sink. No one fussed over anything. Peg would wake each morning, walk the dog, go to a yoga class, buy something for dinner, and tend her garden. Afternoons were spent on the beach reading the latest book club book. Late afternoons were for watching the sunset and sipping a glass of wine while waiting for Rick to drive in and have dinner. Her heart would jump every time he pulled in, and her stomach would ache if he was late. The fear of something happening to him made her body numb. This was a fear she had always had and tried so hard to overcome.

They were there every summer, meeting new people and enjoying life at the beach. They would boat, enjoy the beach, and get away from the hustle and bustle of Williamston.

Peg decorated it like a typical beach house. Bright blues, yellow, and seashells everywhere. Once, she and Rick spent an entire weekend in the yard, pulling weeds and making room for new plantings. At the end of the weekend, there they sat, mud from head to toe, happily sipping a cold beer, filled with the satisfaction of what they had accomplished. Sort of like a lotus flower being nurtured by the muck of the swamp and blooming as beautiful as ever.

The ocean was bluer than blue, the days were lazy and relaxed, there was nowhere to go and nothing to worry about. She would reconnect with friends at the pool where conversations would pick up right where they left off the previous season, as if time had stopped. Friends and neighbors would gather for the annual Memorial Day brunch and look forward to all the social events of the season. Time truly stopped on Pointe Verde in their quiet neighborhood on the river. How carefree those days seem as she now navigates so much. How easy and simple life was when all she had to worry about was preparing the next meal or where to go to the beach for the day.

Memories were built there. Friendships formed for a lifetime. Pointe Verde was Rick's favorite place to be, his "Happy Place." You could see the stress melt away as soon as he crossed the bridge. Whatever was going on in their lives, be it work or personal, they could always count on the tranquility of the ocean to bring peace and calm back into their world. Peace and calm would become Peg's mantra for years to come. She would remind herself daily that peace and calm would be needed to navigate each day and the changes to the life she once knew.

Pointe Verde was a life of pure family time. A time she wanted to last forever. The four of them together for three whole months with no interruptions of school schedules and "things to do." BBQ's, lunch dates, and boating together down the beautiful river. She will always treasure those innocent days. No one can take that time away.

Time, she found out, was so precious. What we do with time is so important. How we spend it, and who we spend it with are choices to make carefully. A day can change in a blink, and you never want to regret how you spent that day.

Chapter 3

SUMMER **2017**

The kids were young adults now; how fast that went by. Instead of riding together to summer on Pointe Verde, the kids drove their own cars to the beach this year. They too always looked forward to enjoying the lazy days of Pointe Verde life—a life they were always grateful for. A life that was simple, not over the top; a life they built together.

That summer, the summer of 2017, was one of the best summers ever. Everyone was in a good place. Rick would take long vacations and work long hours to make his weekends longer. They were beginning to feel what it would be like to be empty nesters and how it would be to truly enjoy the company and friendship they had built over the past twenty-seven years.

Rick bought a convertible, which Peg thought was ridiculous. They would spin around in the small black Audi A4 all summer. They went to the beach, restaurants, watched amazing sunsets, went to outdoor bars, wonderful dinners….laughing, boating, golfing, spending time with beach friends and family; enjoying every minute with their two kids.

Their daughter, Katherine, was entering her senior year at college and Peter was to begin his freshman year at college. Katherine was so excited about the year ahead. So many exciting things to look forward to. Senior dances, parties, and moving into a house with eight of her best friends. Mostly she was excited that Rick and Peg had decided to rent an apartment close by in Port St. Louis. "Senior year of college is the best time of your life," Peg would tell her. "Remember every minute of it, and have fun!!"

Peter was entering a new chapter of his life. Saying goodbye to his small sheltered high school and moving five hours away to begin his college career. He would be playing lacrosse in the spring, and they were excited to see him on the field. He had grown up so much that summer and become so independent, which is always bittersweet for any parent. Peter was a strong man and proved that repeatedly during the next several months. Rick and Peg encouraged him to study hard, make great friends, and do well in lacrosse. They promised to be at every game come spring. But, sadly, that never happened.

With the kids in good places, it was easy to look forward to becoming empty nesters. They would once again be alone with their dog. In the beginning, they had been married seven years while trying desperately to have a baby, with multiple failed attempts. Infertility was the hardest time of their lives. From personal experience, Peg knew it could make or break a marriage. She had seen it in her own marriage and in those of friends. But she and Rick stuck by each other, and Rick, always so positive, never gave up hope they would have the family they longed for.

When they decided to adopt, it was scary but they knew in their hearts it was the right thing to do. Katherine and Peter were born across the world and came into their lives. They would have it no other way. These were the kids meant for them, and a family was formed out of PURE LOVE!

As that final summer of life on Pointe Verde (as they knew it) was coming to an end, Peg watched her son pack to leave for college. Their kids were their lives and now they were both leaving for their own life at college. Young adults ready to conquer the world; their worlds soon to be changed forever. Funny how life goes along and "Bam," you are swept off your feet by love, a child born and adopted into your family, anniversaries that bring great joy, deaths of loved ones, and accidents that were never expected to happen. Great joys and worst fears sweep us off our feet and take our breath away.

As she said goodbye to her son, she was reminded of the day he was put into her arms. Memories flooded her brain; the smell of his head, baby giggles, his first steps, his first word, his small arms around her neck, and so much more. Katherine and Peter were the joy of their lives.

Peg always knew she was blessed with a life of comfort in so many ways. But she never took this for granted and always knew, from the time she was a little girl, that money could never replace happiness, especially if someone you love leaves forever. Her father always told her, "Your health is your wealth."

She also knew that everyone is exactly the same, regardless of what they have or don't have. When your health is threatened, you realize the value of life, and how quickly it can be taken away.

Sure, Rick and Peg had their differences, struggles, and fragile times, but nothing could have prepared Peg for the complete loss of her husband, her confidante, her best friend, her ROCK!!

Chapter 4

♥

The cool breeze of the fall season swept in; sweaters were brought out. Fall was her favorite season of the year. A welcome change, always. A cleanliness in the air. This fall was going to bring so much change to their lives. They were about to pack up the beach house to move into an apartment in Port St. Louis. This would be the start of a life that Rick would not remember. Before she knew it, October 1st arrived and they were moving into an apartment in the city. A city Peg knew very little about, had no friends in, and where everything was unfamiliar. She packed up the convertible and Justice, the dog, and left to meet Rick there. The entire way she was questioning if this was the right thing to do. Selling the house, getting rid of everything they had spent years accumulating, letting go of things they did not use or need. She felt a numbness run through her body, never having imagined she would end up living in a city. She had secretly always wanted to, so maybe this was a manifestation that was coming to realization.

She pulled up to the bright yellow house and started unloading the car, hesitantly walking the three flights of stairs, thinking to herself the entire time that this was a huge mistake but trusting all would be okay. "All is exactly how it is supposed to be, all is perfect in the moment," her mantra.

The apartment was in an old home that had been beautifully renovated. She immediately purged it of all the tacky knickknacks and made it as much like home as possible without decoration or furniture of her own. She put everything in a closet, purchased new pillows and bedding, added some favorite accessories from home, and quickly filled the apartment with photos of family and friends to remind her of the people she loved and trusted.

That night, dinner confirmed they had made the right choice in moving to Port St. Louis. Being closer to work helped alleviate the stress Rick had been under from driving three hours a day.

Peg woke the next morning in Rick's arms in a strange bedroom. It was strange to wake in a room that was not hers; no decor similar to the kind she loved, old lamps and dark walls, the sounds of cars and horns outside, and a bus squeaking to a halt. She looked at Rick who was still sleeping and thought to herself…this is all we need, each other, and life is okay. Unfamiliar surroundings were okay with Rick there to protect her and guide her. He was her strength; her reason for being there and her happiness—but she would quickly be reminded that we are in charge of our own happiness and in charge of our own destiny. No one else, not even those we feel closest to and the most secure around. She would often think of this in the year to come and for the rest of her life.

The area they moved to was a community in Port St. Louis made up of small shops and restaurants. A small community within a larger city sector. It felt like home; coffee shops with outdoor tables, friendly shop owners, and a small bookstore with reading clubs to join. It was comfortable, safe, and friendly. Everything was within walking distance.

Each morning Rick would leave with a kiss and "I love you." Starting the day alone, her first day in Port St. Louis, Peg wondered what to do. She got on the computer and found a yoga studio, ready to jump into a new community that was familiar and comfortable, no matter where she was. The class was great, and she came back to the apartment ready to start her new life.

The phone rang. It was Rick and instead of, "What's for dinner," he said, "So, where are we going for dinner?" So it began, a life in a city where no one knew her name. But it did not matter because she had her best friend by her side every night.

They seemed to do everything they wanted to while living in Port St. Louis. Every night was a new restaurant. Rick would call from work, "Where are we going tonight," and each restaurant was better than the other. Peg started drinking French martinis and whiskey, feeling very cosmopolitan. It was a time of pure fun, almost honeymooning again. Living fast and furious, enjoying every day and night. Long Sunday morning walks, or runs on the boulevard with Justice, brunch with Bloody Marys, not a care in the world. They even squeezed in a week in Florida. Their life was a true love story.

Time got ahead of them and needed to stop for a while—life would pause and change forever. Perhaps if they had a crystal ball, they would have seen it coming. But who really knows what tomorrow will bring? Live life in the present moment…that is all that we have. The past is over, and the future is not real.

Chapter 5

♥

SOUL MATES

Peg was from a blue-collar, working-class family. Her dad and mom raised their children in a lovely home her dad built on the farm where he grew up. She remembers the view from the kitchen of that brown, colonial home. Land as far as she could see. A small barn in the distance with woods behind it. A pine tree in their pretty yard. In the winters there would be a blanket of snow. They lived simply. Winters were spent sledding on the hill behind their home. Summers were spent with family and friends in the neighborhood and in the backyard running under a sprinkler. A big outing and true treat was going to the beach for a day.

Peg's dad worked long hours every day in construction and grew a small business to support his family. There were no vacations growing up, no summer homes, or fancy cars.

Peg's family had strong Italian traditions and created lasting memories at Sunday dinners. Her mom would start frying meatballs at 8:00 am on Sundays. Peg will always remember the smell of her family's home and the memories of those crazy dinners.

Her parents' home was one where anyone was welcome to stop in at any time. There would always be a fresh pot of coffee and something to eat. It did not matter what the house looked like. It was the warm greeting her parents gave to anyone who stopped by that mattered most.

Even though money was tight, her parents made sure Peg went to the best private school in the area. It was a small Catholic school that brought the community together. Peg's mom worked there, and her dad put in driveways for free so Peg could attend the school. As a shy girl, it was the perfect place for her. There she formed friendships and confidence. It was at this school where she first laid eyes on Rick, the cutest boy she ever saw!

They say people are put in your life for a reason. Peg's best friend in first grade was a girl named Susan. Susan was half Peg's size but was a feisty girl who was bossy, confident, and full of life. The two were inseparable. The first time Susan invited Peg to her home, Peg thought she was at the White House. It was a beautiful white home overlooking the entire city! Peg lived in a beautiful home, but this was something she had never seen. A grand foyer with an elevator and rooms upon rooms, spiral staircases, big and beautiful. It was quiet and perfect, nothing out of place. There were playdates and sleepovers often. One birthday party, in walked Rick, Susan's cousin. They were in grade school and instantly Peg's eyes went to him. She thought he was the cutest boy she had ever seen, not knowing years later she would fall in love with and marry him.

Upon graduating from college, Peg found herself driving to a party where Rick wanted her to meet him. The home was spectacular, overlooking the water. It was the summer home where he grew up, and a place he would want for his own family someday. She met his family; a large family of six kids and cousins upon cousins. The family she would later marry into. This family, opposite from her world in every way, yet, with strong family values and love for each other, as her own family valued so much. The strong love and family values their parents impressed upon them would hold them tightly together. It held Peg and Rick together during the years to come as they would face the biggest challenges a married couple could endure.

Five years later, there she was, walking down the aisle. And there he was, waiting at the altar to begin a life together. A life filled with love and challenges she never expected.

As they began their marriage, it was carefree. Lots of good times together, dates with friends, travel, and general freedom and fun that young couples without children enjoy. They knew they wanted children, but in the beginning, they enjoyed their time together, just the two of them.

Infertility was a challenge that hit them head on. This is a time when many couples fall apart; however, Peg and Rick found themselves even closer, supporting and comforting each other through many long nights of tears. Wanting children so badly; they tried for seven years without a pregnancy. But it was not a pregnancy she wanted; she wanted a child. They decided to adopt, and a beautiful baby girl was sent to them from across the world and two years later, a beautiful baby boy...their family was complete.

Chapter 6

RICK'S STRENGTH

Rick was working later and later; it was a busy time of year and sales were good. He loved his job and his friends at work and everything that went with it. He was high on the corporate ladder after working very hard for thirty-three years to get there. Peg made their life smooth and easy by bringing up the kids, handling their schooling, sports, carpools, and playdates. Rick did not have to worry about a thing on the home front.

The love Rick had for Peg and the kids was amazing. He was the type of man that balanced his time well. He never missed one of his son's hockey games or his daughter's soccer games. He would always rearrange his busy work schedule for his family, no matter what. He was solid and strong; mentally, spiritually, and physically. He cared deeply about Peg and the kids, and always put them in front of everything and everyone. He always made sure their family unit was strong and safe.

Peg never could explain it, but an overwhelming fear would often flow through her when he would be late getting home or not call. He always thought she was crazy and would calm her by telling her, "Everything is okay…stop your worrying! I love you, and nothing is going to happen!" I guess life seemed almost "too perfect" and she was so afraid of losing it that she almost gripped it too tightly. When you are too attached to anything, you soon find out it will be gone. Nothing, absolutely nothing, in life stays the same. People change, situations change, life changes. Staying present to the day is all that really matters. This was hard to imagine, but, as Peg looks back on her life, it's so damn true. We are constantly in change—and you cannot hold tightly to anything. Be GRATEFUL for the moment, the time, and the way things are in the moment, whether good or bad, it too will pass; it will be gone!

Chapter 7

♥

TIME STOPS: PORT ST. LOUIS, TUESDAY, JANUARY 24TH, 2017

Peg heard his alarm go off. "Shit, it's so early!" It was 6:00 am; a rainy, snowy mix of precipitation falling outside. Justice jumped on the bed and Peg put her head under the covers pretending to still be asleep. She heard Rick get out of the warm bed, turn the shower on, and get himself ready for a long day of meetings ahead. His entire sales team was in town, and he was excited to have them all together. The day would be long but he would reward them with a great team dinner that night. Peg knew this was a big deal and Rick looked forward to it each year. Yet, part of her was annoyed at the whole thing. She would be left alone in this apartment she was trying to call home with no one around to call or go out with.

When she heard the shower turn off, she got herself out of bed and took Justice outside for a quick pee. Climbing the stairs to their second-floor apartment she felt cold. A cold feeling she had never felt before. A feeling that makes you want to get back in bed and curl up and let the day go away and begin again tomorrow. A feeling like she just did not want the day to begin.

She put on the coffee and sipped it as she waited for Rick to come out of the bedroom. He was dressed up, and his smell would linger long after he was gone. It was a clean scent, a handsome and strong scent. Putting on his coat as he was running a little late, something he hated to do, he gave Justice a quick pat on the head and leaned over to Peg, giving her a kiss goodbye. "I love you," she said. "Love you, too. I will call you on my way to dinner." She said okay and the door slammed. She went to the window, something she never did, and watched him clear off his beautiful Audi A8, his pride and joy. As he waited for it to warm up, he checked his phone, then his seat belt went on, and off he drove. She still felt that cold feeling as she walked away from the window, and for some reason, climbed back into bed, closing her eyes and meditating on the moment. She grabbed her daily journal and wrote:

"Today I am opening my heart to be more compassionate and trusting to those I love most. I am going to open my heart to new people I meet, and all life's opportunities. I'm opening to new possibilities to teach here in Port St. Louis and making that happen. I am opening my heart and will live through love and compassion. Grateful for the walk I had with Ricky over the weekend, grateful for the friends in my life, and grateful for my two beautiful, amazing kids!"

Wow! As she looks back, she realizes the universe was preparing her for what she would lose, what she would gain, and who would be there along the way.

She looked at Justice and said, "Okay, let's get this day started!" After putting on her rain gear, she took him for a five-mile walk. She walked down the street and then to the boulevard, where just two days ago she and Rick walked together. On her way back to the apartment she stopped for coffee. She dried off the dog and took a long shower. Sitting at the counter wondering what to do next, she shot her daughter a text. "Want to grab Sushi tonight? Dad is out, we can have some girl time." She was grateful Katherine lived two miles away. "So there," she said to the dog, "I do have a plan for tonight."

Katherine arrived around 5:00 pm and they chatted about her life at school, her friends, her classes, and all she was looking forward to for the spring of her senior year. They then ventured out for dinner. Arriving back home at 7:00 pm, she asked Katherine to sleep over, never having done that before. But Katherine had to get back to finish some homework and Peg understood. Peg kissed her goodbye and told her they would see her over the weekend. Happy as a clam,

Katherine's world was right where it needed to be; safe and sound, everything in place—for now.

Pouring a glass of wine and getting into her sweats, Peg went into the living room with Justice and put on a show she and Rick had been watching together. When the phone rang it was Rick.

"Hey…walking to the restaurant, meeting the team, I won't be late." A little annoyed because she was alone in the apartment, Peg sighed. "Okay, see you later tonight," she responded. Those were the last words they would speak to each other for several months.

Peg looked at her phone at 10:00 pm and noticed a text message from John, one of Rick's dearest friends from work, which alerted her that something was wrong. She saw she had also missed a call from the hospital and her body began to go numb. She called John who told her Rick had been hit by a car, he didn't know anything more. She called the hospital and was told to come immediately. Peg fell on the ground and froze. She felt pain, sorrow, and denial all at once. But it was the numbness she often felt when fear set in that was paralyzing her entire body from her toes up her legs, into her torso, stomach, back, arms, head, and like a dagger straight into her heart and lungs, taking her breath away. She was there on the floor and could not move. Peg was in a state of shock. She sat on the floor for what felt like hours. Her phone rang, snapping her back to reality. It was John. "I don't know what to do John, I can't move," she said. He would be the first of many guardian angels whom God would send to bring her comfort.

John said, "Put the dog in a room, get your purse and medical ID cards, and go wait in front of the apartment." Justice, OMG, her dog, where was he? On the floor next to her, of course, as if he knew something terrible was wrong. Justice looked at her and placed his head on her lap. She remembered getting him as a small puppy and knowing he would bring so much joy to their lives. Rick adored him. With tears rolling down her face, she looked at him and said, "Go to your room, I will be back." Justice sat in silence, staring at her with fear in his eyes. After giving him a bowl of water, she closed the door. It would be four weeks before she saw him again.

As she was packing to leave the apartment, Peg phoned her sister who lived four hours away on Island Shoals. "Sara, Rick is in the hospital, he was hit by a car. I know nothing. I am heading there. I have no one to call, no one is answering their phones, what do I do?" Before she finished the story, Sara and her husband Bill were in the car. Sara knew she had to get there to be with Peg and Rick.

An Uber driver John had called pulled up. John stayed with her on the line the whole way to the hospital despite being two hours away. The hospital was three miles away, but the ride seemed like three hours. As she sobbed, the driver, a complete stranger, tried to offer comfort. When he dropped her off he looked at her. A young man probably her own son's age. He looked at her and said, "God bless you; I am sure your husband will be alright." The second angel that night who appeared to offer her comfort and reinforce her faith in God.

FAMILIAR HELL

She walked into the cold emergency room. Familiar smells of the hospital quickly brought her back to six years earlier when her parents were in the ER, a time she wanted to block out forever. People were everywhere, and she just wanted to find Rick and be with him. Peg went to the desk and explained, "I received a phone call, my husband Rick." "Rick who?," said the cold receptionist. "MY HUSBAND, where is he?" she shouted. Just at that point a social worker appeared and asked Peg to follow her to the trauma unit where her husband was. They took the elevator to the 5th floor. The social worker took her to a waiting room and offered her tea or water, which Peg declined, and told her to wait there. She said the trauma staff was with Rick and it would be a while.

As Peg waited in the COLD room, she began calling Rick's siblings, knowing they needed to be there for their brother, but no one answered. She was frantically leaving messages. After what seemed like hours, someone finally came to explain that Rick had been struck by a car, but she could not see him yet. "Was there anyone she could call to sit with her?" the nurse asked. At that moment Peg broke down in tears. The reality was she knew not one person in Port St. Louis (other than her daughter) to call. And there was no way she could call Katherine until she knew what she was facing. Though it took all her strength not to pick up the phone and call her.

Little did she know that over the next months she would gain a network of 300 people she would call "family." These people surrounded her and her children with so much love and support.

Her phone rang and it was Rick's oldest sister, Jane, who she spoke with until Sara arrived almost two hours later. Jane would not hang up; she stayed with Peg until Sara arrived.

When Sara arrived the two of them fell into each other's arms. Peg's sister would be her anchor as she blindly went through the next hours, months, and years ahead. Even though Sara was younger, Peg had always admired her strength, courage, independence, and confidence to make it on her own. Peg was always sheltered. Her parents never gave her the confidence she needed to go out and do anything on her own. Sure she went off to Burlington and away to school, but nothing she did really seemed to impress upon anyone. She was the pretty face who no one really took seriously. Now she was thrown into a situation where she had to handle everything for everyone, as well as make decisions that were life changing for Rick and the kids. She would be asked to sign documents and medical releases daily. She had to keep it together as best she knew how; this she would absolutely make sure of.

As they waited together, few words were spoken—she was petrified. There was what felt like a hole in her heart, as if someone was crushing her lungs. Her arms were numb, and she could not take a deep breath. Her heart was beating out of her chest and she felt like she was going to puke. It was so overwhelming!! Breathe, she kept telling herself, just as she often told her yoga students. Your breath will bring you to the present moment and calm you. That's what she would do from this day forward for the rest of her life. She would now operate on the premise of knowing that the past is over, the future does not yet exist, and the present is what is real. Although this all seemed like a horrible nightmare, it was real and this was happening, and somehow, she would have to navigate her way through it and not be paralyzed by fear.

Walking into the room to see Rick was a nightmare. She nearly collapsed on top of his swollen body. The strong, handsome man she knew and loved looked like a monster. He was totally disfigured. His head and body were swollen; he had tubes everywhere. One in his head to monitor brain activity and pressure, one in his throat to help him to breath, two in his chest, one in his stomach, and another in his groin. It was heartbreaking. She did not look at anything except his eyes, which were closed. She clasped his left hand and kissed his bloody forehead and leaned toward his ear and said with a whisper, "Ricky, I am here." At that moment she saw a tear roll down his cheek. In the background, as if miles away, she heard doctors and nurses and even her sister and brother-in-law yelling at Rick to open his eyes and give a thumbs up. She whispered to him again, "Give a thumbs up, Ricky, if you can hear me?" At that point his left thumb went up and she was convinced he would come back to her.

"OPEN YOUR EYES, RICK, GIVE A THUMBS UP," would be shouted constantly during the next seven weeks. It would be shouted at 5:00 am when the doctors did rounds and shouted again every time a nurse or doctor would come into the room. She would watch, and day after day there would be no response from Rick. He just laid there, a shell with machines keeping his body alive. Neurologists would come in and tell her he *would* open his eyes, but when and how were a mystery. Not knowing was the worst nightmare. This is when living minute by minute was so important.

Her beautiful, handsome husband was broken. His back was broken, his leg was broken, his lungs collapsed, and his head smashed. His beautiful blue eyes would not open for seven weeks, and he would not breathe completely on his own for the same length of time. His heart and blood pressure were all over the map. It was horrific, an image she would hopefully be able to erase one day.

She stayed with him all night, her sister by her side. The morning light finally came, and she immediately tried to call the kids, leaving messages that they must call her. Oh God, how would she ever be able to tell them this? How was she to comfort them when she needed comfort herself?

But Katherine and Peter were her true comfort through it all. They would arrive that day, understandably devastated. She remembers Katherine. The elevator opened and she fell into Peg's arms, sobbing and shaking. Peg held her tight and told her everything was going to be okay. "I promise," she said. "Everything is scary right now, but it will be okay." She walked Katherine to her father's hospital room. When Katherine walked in and saw her hero broken, she fell into Peg once again. They cried together. Then this beautiful, young woman who just hours before went to bed safe, knowing all was well, sat by her father's side. Perched in the corner of his hospital room, day after day with her computer, never leaving his side. Her senior year of college was not what she had expected.

Peter arrived soon after Katherine. He traveled four hours not knowing what to expect. He entered silently, saw everyone in the waiting room and went to Peg. Together they walked into Rick's room, and he fell apart. This strong boy who was almost a man with so much ahead of him crumbled. His father, his confidante, his ROCK was gone. Over the next several months Peter would make that long four hour drive every weekend to be by her side, offering advice and wisdom. Helping with major medical and financial decisions. Helping his mother; stepping into Rick's shoes knowing exactly what his father would expect him to do.

The three of them clung to each other during those weeks in the trauma unit. Together they watched every monitor and every move Rick made. In that apartment in Port St. Louis, they hugged each other tight. Comforting one another; hoping, hoping, and hoping. Life would never be the same again for their family, and they knew it.

The next several hours and days were a blur. Doctors shouting orders and nurses monitoring levels. Medical decisions had to be made quickly and Peg had to sign for each operation and every procedure. Trusting in the doctors. Peter told her to listen to the doctors, NO ONE else!! And that is exactly what she did. Keep breathing she told herself; be strong for these kids but know it's okay not to be okay. Deep, deep down Peg knew it would all fall into place, because that is what Rick always told her. "Don't worry, everything will fall into place," he always said.

Chapter 8

Looking Back, Two Days Prior

Peg was so excited—they were going to a black-tie affair with their dearest friends, Dan and Barbara, friends from high school. They shared many significant events together; marriages, engagement parties, family parties, milestone birthdays, etc. Their kids were best friends, too. They lived two doors down on Pointe Verde.

Rick was as handsome as ever in his black tie. She wore her black Armani dress, a classic she had worn to several events. Other than Dan and Barbara, they did not know anyone at the event, but they had each other and that was all that mattered. They arrived at the country club and looked over the silent auction items. There was an overnight stay at a resort and spa. Peg immediately bid on this and ended up winning it—not realizing the room would be used for one of Rick's aides when they attended their niece's wedding several months later.

They drank, laughed, and danced. Peg remembers their last dance together. Rick held her a little closer and a little tighter than he normally did. *Wonderful Tonight* by Eric Clapton played—she did not want it to end. She felt so safe, so loved and secure in his strong arms. He kissed her gently when the song was over and whispered, "You look beautiful, I love you."

Whenever he held her in his arms, Peg could feel all of his positive energy and felt completely safe and secure. That night at the charity ball, as he held her, she melted like a schoolgirl. Every time he held her, she fell deeper and deeper in love with him—her confidante and her best friend.

They had a great time that evening with Dan and Barbara, and with each other. Dan and Barbara had always been there for them, in good times and not so good times, as Peg and Rick had been for Dan and Barbara. It was a constant friendship, and over the years ahead Dan and Barbara were right by their side, offering whatever was needed to help Peg navigate through the darkest days of her life.

The next day was a rainy, cold day but Rick wanted to go for a run after brunch. He returned refreshed and feeling great—his last run for the rest of his life.

Every August they ran a road race together to raise funds for cystic fibrosis. Rick never missed a chance to raise funds for CF when possible.

That is what Rick did. He believed in people. Lifted them up instead of tearing them down. Never saying a bad word about anyone. Always living with the glass half full, positive in every way possible. He was always willing to help anyone he could. Rick was the type of husband, father, friend, boss, brother, and son you could always count on to offer sound advice, no matter what you were going through. He would listen with his heart and speak the truth. Rick was one of the most authentic guys Peg had ever met.

Rick was not a big shot talker. He never boasted about anything. He was humble and kind, and often kept his thoughts to himself. If he did not have something productive or positive to say, he was quiet. Often people thought he was a little snobbish…but soon they loved him for his true self. He was strong and confident. Never caring what anyone thought of him. He was completely confident in his own skin. Never pretending to be anyone else, and never in competition with anyone.

Chapter 9

Angels

It's been said that if you are open to signs from heaven or the universe, you will become aware and be able to see angels showing up in your life. That is exactly what happened to Peg. During Rick's hospitalization and long recovery, friends, family, and strangers showed up for Peg and their children in ways she never could have expected. Peg came to think of these special people as her "angels."

The first angel to appear in Peg's life was her father. Ever since her father died, six years prior to Rick's accident, he showed up when she needed him most. He came to her through music and ladybugs. Every time she needed his comfort, he would appear. She was comforted by his presence through these signs. Her father once told her that as long as he was with her, she never needed to be scared. Physically he was gone, but his presence was there with her all the time.

Nurses and doctors constantly appeared in Rick's hospital room. Strangers she would come to know by name and think of as angels. She would rely on them for comfort. She knew they would give Rick comfort. She would trust completely in the decisions they made for her husband.

As each new ICU nurse came in for their shift, it seemed they were sent at the exact time she needed them. As if God was sending them one by one. She remembers Andrea (at first Andrea seemed to be all business), the one who always told her Rick was going to wake up and would be okay. She was all business in her treatment but knew what he needed. There was Juan who walked in one day to care for Rick and Peg ended up sobbing in his arms. He took care of her for the day.

Whether it was the comfort of one or the sternness of another, they were all sent to care for Rick at the time he needed them to be there. As each day passed and days ran into nights and weeks ran into months, nurses, aides, doctors, respiratory therapists, even janitors were there to guide her in the right direction. From the first night, sitting alone with a social worker who comforted her as she waited to see Rick, to each new nurse who came in to ease her worrying heart or work on Rick, they were all angels sent at just the right time.

Angels also appeared in the ICU waiting room, too. The waiting room was dark with ripped leather chairs and a smell that lingered. Every time the elevator opened everyone would stare at the new stranger entering this madness, this room of fear and tragedy.

Yet it became a place of support, with strangers giving strangers love and comfort. It was a place where strangers cried together, hugged one another, and prayed together. At first, greeting each other with a timid smile, but soon hugging. Peg remembers the families who came in, sitting and waiting to see their loved ones. Looking back, Peg realized we are all truly connected in this world. Every person in the ICU, from different races, cultures, and socioeconomic backgrounds had a common pain, and hurt. They all felt their heart was broken, an ache so deep, and a fear that numbed every bone and muscle in their body. Each had a loved one in the care of this amazing unit. They were all connected and held captive in this small waiting room.

Peg began comforting others, not even realizing she was doing it. Later in the day or early in the morning, especially, these people seemed so familiar to her. The daughter with her father across the hall from Rick who wrote Peg a note saying, "These two men are the strongest men I know. I hope you find peace." Her father had fallen from a roof and suffered a major stroke. He fought day and night to come back to his friends and family. Derrick was his name, he was Rick's age and he and Rick were in a coma for weeks, everyone shouting, "OPEN YOUR EYES, MOVE A FINGER." These two families and men were connected beyond belief.

Derrick left the hospital before Rick. He left in a coma and died several months later. Leaving behind his beautiful daughter, young son, and so many friends. These friends became her friends. A connection was formed. They would come into Rick's room and offer comfort to her. God connected these two worlds, and they would remain forever connected by LOVE.

There was a young man, thirty years old, who came in late one night, his wife rushed in after delivering their first child. He did not know where to turn. Peg sat there looking at him. She retrieved her rosary beads and gave them to him. "I will pray for you," she said. He had no words, just a long hug. Months later she would run into this same young man in the rehab parking lot. His wife had been sent to rehab and Peg had met her. Such a young couple with so much faith and LOVE to help them move through their pain.

Peg came to fully understand that we are all connected and one. There really are no differences between people. Humanity is one with LOVE. Hearts break the same way whenever a loved one falls ill. The ache in the heart is so strong and so similar for everyone. And everyone needs those angels that Peg found in that waiting room.

Everyone she met offered a glimmer of hope in their own way. Each person was a comfort, and one by one they were there for her as she watched Rick's body slowly heal. First the swelling in his chest and face went down. The head wound began to fade a little, his breathing became steadier with the help of the ventilator, his hands were healing. His broken leg was repaired and casted, his back operated on, and a steel rod put in, a permanent reminder of what had happened.

After weeks, Rick had shown no movement. Some were rushing him to recovery, asking questions no one could answer. There seemed to be constant chatter and lines of people coming and going, which Peg knew must be stopped. PEG KNEW WHAT HER HUSBAND NEEDED. HE NEEDED HER TO BE THERE AND NO ONE ELSE. SHE NEEDED TO PUT A STOP TO ALL THE VISITORS COMING AND GOING. She needed all computers, cell phones, and chatter stopped and taken out of his room.

After weeks of Rick being there it was becoming too much for her to handle. Not only did she need to put all her attention on Rick, but she also needed to manage her children's needs. The added task of answering questions from friends and family, questions she had no answers to, was just too much. She decided she needed to be ALONE, and that Rick needed QUIET!! Everyone knew it was important to talk to Rick, but he really did not care what was going on in the news, sports, or anything else. What he needed to hear was Peg's voice! Telling him about their life, the kid's lives, and ensuring him she was okay, but also admitting to him how fucking scared she really was. She needed to cry and tremble with fear next to him with NO ONE coming into the room. She needed to beg him for guidance. She needed to NOT BE OKAY!!! She needed to come apart! Rick needed to hear from her. Everyone kept telling him she was okay, that they were watching out for her—he needed to hear she was NOT okay!! Because that was the truth! She was scared to death! Their kids were scared to death. They were taking care of each other! That was the truth! He needed to hear that in order to come back to them.

Peg politely asked everyone to leave them alone for two weeks. She assured them she was fine, the kids were fine, and that Rick needed this time of quiet to try to wake up. She pulled out her yoga and meditation tools and put them in place. Breathing deeply, quieting things around her, staying present, getting rid of the stories, etc. She dimmed the lights in the room, brought in healing crystals, played meditation music, and did not let go of Rick's hand. She talked to him softly, played music, sang, and told him about the kids and what was going on, without any interruption. She knew what needed to be done in order for his eyes to open and for him to respond. She did not care who did or did not understand this...this was the way she wanted it. Taking all she learned from her yoga practice and trusting in God, she moved through two weeks of being alone with her husband. Soft music and meditation sounds were played daily for two full weeks, and Rick slowly began to come back to her. He opened his eyes, raised a thumb, and moved his toe. At the end of these quiet weeks, he would begin rehab that would last the rest of his life.

Rehab began in the form of simply trying to raise Rick up with full support. He had been in bed for two full months, not moving a muscle. Next came sitting on the edge of the bed with full support. She remembers the touch of his hand on her back, and how grateful she was for his light touch again. Every night a tear rolled down his face. She assured him, and promised him, all would be okay. Every day was the same—up at 5:00 am to be at the hospital at 5:30 so she could be there for rounds. Watching the monitors as his blood pressure spiked, his heart rate was erratic, blood draining, temperature rising and falling. Tubes were everywhere; it was all so terrifying. Praying in the chapel which at first felt like a Rubik's Cube, cold and lonely. But it soon became a safe haven for her to be alone. Whenever she was not in Rick's room, she was in the chapel, praying her rosary. The angels kept coming in the wee hours of the morning and into the late evening hours. Just when her body and spirit were crumbling, an angel would appear and take the fear away, giving her a bit of strength to move forward.

Chapter 10

A Message From God

One night at 11:00 pm Peg received a phone call from a complete stranger. He had heard from a friend of Rick's about the accident. The man's name was Will. She had no idea what to think, but something told her she needed to hear what this man had to say. As she hovered over Rick's broken body, Will told her to trust in God's healing. After she hung up, she cried and told Rick, "God has this. We cannot control what is going to happen, so I am trusting He will get us through this in his own way. We cannot question why anymore." That night she woke at 3:30 am in the recliner by Rick's bed. She left his room and wandered the halls of the hospital with a blanket wrapped around her, thinking she was caught in the worst nightmare ever and feeling like she was having a complete nervous breakdown. For some reason she started to think about her dad. While in the cafeteria a song came on the radio. She knew instantly her dad was the angel that night. Walking those cold halls with her, giving her the courage she needed to take the elevator back upstairs and enter Rick's room. Her angel that night, her dad, helped her find strength and resilience to get her family through that dark time.

The next angels sent to her were their kids. The kids became her strength at this point. They were angels God sent to help her move forward and prevent her from falling into a dark hole. They were there every weekend. Katherine sat in the corner of the room. Peg could only imagine what she was thinking. Peter, taking charge, leading the way, holding his dad's hand and talking him through—crying the whole way back to school, she was sure. Their lives had been flipped upside down, changed, and affected in a way they never would have imagined. But Rick taught them all to stay strong, stay together, be confident, and positive. And that is what they were trying so hard to do.

These two children, who were sent to them from across the ocean, were exactly where they were supposed to be. They knew they had to stay true to Rick and Peg, but also to themselves. The four of them drew courage and strength from one another each day.

ONE DAY AT A TIME and one breath at a time. Remember, you can handle anything in the moment, it is our fear of what might happen that undoes us. This is what hours of yoga training and practice had taught Peg.

When she started yoga, years before Rick's devastating accident, it was so freeing. When she was asked to teach, it was as if it were meant to be. She remembers her cousin, Jenna, calling her.

Jena was opening a yoga studio and asked Peg, "Would you ever consider teaching yoga, Peg?"

"Oh my God, I would love to, do you really think I can?"

"Of course!" Jena said. "I would love for you to teach. I can help train you."

Peg hung up the phone, opened her email, and there it was, the universe coming in loud and clear, a teacher training course was coming to her area! She clicked on the link and registered. Not knowing what to expect, she trusted this was meant to happen.

One Day At A Time

How Peg walked through this storm she never fully understood. At first it felt like an out of body experience, not real, just going through days that all blended together. As time went on, Peg realized this was real. This was her new life, Rick's new life, and her children's new life. It may not have been what they would have chosen, but it was now theirs.

She was alone, but never truly alone. She had to navigate through the day-to-day business of their lives. Meeting with people she didn't know in order to understand how to manage their life without it falling apart.

She sat up nights thinking things through and decided one thing at a time; one meeting at a time; one phone call at a time; one decision at a time. Trying to stay clear in each task. Her mantra was, "ONE DAY AT A TIME." Pieces began to fall into place and healing began for her family!

They were truly "Team Rock," a couple whose love and support was healing their broken life. It was this love that brought them through infertility, a love that would continue to grow, change, and shape who they were as a couple and a family.

The kids were angry, sad, and confused by the absence of their parents. One day at a time meant making sure their kids were okay. Calling them, asking friends and family to watch out for them. Trying to be with them as often as possible.

One day at a time meant calling insurance people and lawyers and working through all the paperwork that came along with this trauma. One day at a time meant keeping in touch with friends as much as possible and trying to maintain somewhat of a normal routine for herself. Despite these attempts, she found her sense of self slipping away due to being so caught up in the caregiver routine. She was determined to redirect that immediately.

All along everyone kept saying was, "Take care of yourself." Really? What did that even mean? Going to a spa, getting nails done, eating good food? Really? While her husband lay almost dead in the hospital. No way did that happen! Peg spent every waking moment beside Rick in the ICU and through his stay at rehab. This is what she needed to do and what he needed in order to heal. She was certain of this. So one day at a time meant being by his side every moment of every day, no matter what anyone thought or said to try and stop her from doing exactly that. Day in and day out, this was her life, ONE DAY AT A TIME.

Chapter 11

HEALING

After having looked at nursing care facilities, there was no way Peg would allow her husband to go to one. He was coming home, and that was final.

Leaving the ICU was the scariest thing for Peg. The familiar doctors, nurses, nurse aides, and therapists were no longer going to be with them. Peg had been there every day at 5:00 am and stayed until the wee hours of the night. Now the familiar smells, sounds, faces, and food would be gone. As they wheeled Rick out of his room, she was sobbing...sobbing because they were leaving the safety of this unit and because she did not know what was in store at the next stop on this road to recovery.

They were headed to rehabilitation. She would live in a hotel for six months while Rick went through multiple therapies each day. This meant waking up in a hotel, walking the dog, and going to the building where she watched Rick's PT, OT, and speech therapy. She learned, too, and she took notes on how to manage Rick once he was home. Walking step by step beside Rick until he could balance and do things himself. Putting him in the shower, helping him in and out of bed, learning safe transfers, and making sure she could do it all at home.

As she sat in the ambulance with Rick, memories of riding with her dad to Burlington six years prior in an ambulance flooded her mind. He too had been taken to rehab in Burlington. Her dad, her hero, suffered a massive stroke which left him totally dependent. His beautiful speech was taken, and everything else as well.

People told her this was the best rehab in the world. Sadly, her dad was beyond help and soon had to be moved to a nursing home for a full year. During that year Rick was by Peg's side. He took care of the kids and all the household chores and responsibilities. She disappeared from her own family to care for her father and mother. Peg put her own life on hold in every way. She was with her dad almost daily. She took him outside for long walks, pushing him in a wheelchair for hours. She brought him breakfast, lunch, and sometimes dinner from home in order to be with him. She could not bear to leave him alone. She took over as his guardian since no one else could do it. She took on all his responsibilities and care. She made all his medical decisions. Dealing with doctors and therapists daily. She made legal decisions. She dealt with all his insurance needs. It was all-consuming. Her role shifted that year from mother and wife to caregiver for her father.

Peg looks back now and understands why she had to go through that nightmare. It was to prepare her for this HELL. When they brought her dad into the room which looked out over the city, she couldn't help but notice a beautiful bridge, a structure so close and powerful, so healing and strong that she knew right then she had made the right decision to bring him there.

During that time Peg felt waves of guilt, fear, anger, and complete sadness for her father. Rick and her sister reassured Peg that she was doing the right thing and making all the right decisions. Rick was her ROCK through this most difficult time in her life. He offered her 100% love and comfort.

As Rick's ambulance approached Burlington, there it was, the familiar bridge which would become her guide over the next six months. She would be living in a hotel under the bridge and praying to her dad under it every morning and every night. It would become a beacon of strength and hope in challenging times ahead. It would remind her that she was never alone. Each night, leaving rehab, she would look at the bridge and pray. Each morning she would walk under it and pray again.

So, when the ambulance pulled up to this enormous, beautiful building on the harbor she felt so hopeful. This is where Rick needed to stay until he was able to come home. His room was bright, huge, private, had a huge bathroom, and immediately a team was put into place. A doctor, nurse, and three therapists (physical, occupational, and speech) were assigned to him. This team met Rick at the elevator and got right to work. Assessing him, asking questions, getting him cleaned up, and making him as comfortable as possible. The white board in his room had a schedule for the next day, beginning at 8:00 am. They wasted not a minute of time. Healing was to begin the minute he entered that building.

No one ever said Traumatic Brain Injury (TBI). The doctors told Peg they had no crystal ball as to how or when Rick would heal. They did tell her he *would* wake up, but they could only speculate as to whether he would be Rick, the husband and father he had been. Would he remember the family he loved so much? No one knew the answer.

Peg knew his brain had been affected but she had been so focused on getting him safely out of the trauma unit and to rehab that she did not pay attention. The first time she realized Rick truly had a brain injury was when they got off the elevator at the rehab hospital. The sign said: Brain Injury. Her heart stopped and she could not breathe. She paused when the elevator doors opened, not wanting to step foot on that unit. Rick would be on this unit for the next five and a half months.

Despite her shock and fear, Peg knew she must do what needed to be done, primarily being there for Rick and helping him heal. She met his nurse, a woman from Haiti. She was kind, calm, intelligent, well put together, and offered both Peg and Rick so much more than just nursing care. She was the one angel Peg would call their guide. She spent countless hours with Rick, nursing him calmly back to life. This woman/angel offered hope every single day. And she taught Peg how to care for Rick.

The reality of Rick's injury and the knowledge that he had suffered a TBI hit her the first day there. Rick was unable to answer basic questions. Using a comb or knowing what a cup was for, these things confused Rick. Writing or counting to five, forget it. These were all clear signs Rick's brain was badly affected by this catastrophic event. Never mind the physical limitations, such as walking, sitting up, balancing, transferring, not being able to take food by mouth. She watched him being lifted out of bed with a Hoyer lift and thought to herself, "I don't care about his body, just bring his mind and memories back to me, please." It broke her heart and brought back memories of her father's days in rehab.

Just like her father, the other man and hero she relied on for protection, love, and safety, Rick was torn away from her completely.

Never one to give up hope, she was certain Rick would make progress. Once again, she made the decision to spend every waking day by his side. Being there for every therapy session and learning exactly what they were doing and why. Learning everything she needed to know about TBI. She got to know his doctors, nurses, aides, therapists, social workers, and case managers who walked by his side every day. She wanted to personally know these people, "the angels," who were taking care of her husband. For the second time, putting her life on complete hold, putting their children's lives on hold, as if all their lives would be frozen during this time of complete healing over the next several months. Living day by day...ONE DAY AT A TIME!!

As Rick's mind began to wake up, he was frustrated and agitated to the point that at times she would have to leave the room. He shouted things that were unbearable to hear and acted in odd ways. It was hard to watch, but, thankfully, it passed. Doctors had warned her this may happen. As one becomes aware of the situation, the brain does crazy things. Rick thought he was in a nightmare and shouted at her to wake him up. She was told to leave the room because he had to be allowed to go through this. They never sedated him. He would shout, scream, and cry. She would leave the room, fold up in the waiting room, and sob until he was calm again. But she never left the building until she knew he was okay and sleeping.

And so the healing began, day by day getting stronger and stronger, clearer and clearer. Rick began to sit up, speak, and little by little the IV tubes were removed, and he began to breathe and eat on his own. It was truly a miracle happening in front of her eyes. Peg was filled with hope and days began to make sense. The brain is amazing, and no one knows just how it will heal after a traumatic injury. Peg believed medicine healed the injuries, but knew God was healing Rick's brain and his soul. A broken man was beginning to come together again.

The therapists were amazing, and Peg was awed by their support and their determination to make every minute of rehab count. Three hours every day was like running three marathons for Rick. He was emotionally and physically exhausted.

Peg did not miss a single therapy session. Being right there, observing everything they were doing, was so important to her. She needed to know there was hope. As time went on, she realized there was hope.

Chapter 12

HOTEL HOME

Walking from the hotel to rehab was a straight line along the incredible harbor. Peg walked past the museum each day. This area became her home until she arrived in the lobby of the rehab facility and her body once again became numb as she braced herself to begin the day. A day watching her husband suffer through pain, panic, PT, OT, and speech as he fought to regain some of his life, little by little.

When Rick was moved to rehab, Peg thought she would be staying in the hotel for eight weeks. It turned out to be five and a half months. She arrived at the hotel with Justice and a suitcase of clothes. Her sisters-in-law tried to make this cold place home for her. They brought flowers, food, and pictures of her and Rick.

As she walked the long, dreary hallway that first night, she thought to herself, "This cannot be real." As days moved into weeks and weeks into months, the greetings from the staff were comforting. At first, they were strangers but they soon became friends and family. The love she felt for them was like that she felt for her own family. Each morning they greeted her warmly, and they lovingly said goodnight each evening.

Peg woke early, before sunrise, every day. She got the dog ready and headed to the elevator. Laura at the front desk was always ready with a smile. Jose was ready with a treat for the dog and a grand smile, reminding her to pray. She returned as the sun was coming up. She'd take Justice back to the room, kiss him goodbye, and head downstairs. She grabbed a coffee, and the guys hugged her goodbye.

Arriving back at the hotel late in the evenings, Carly and Greg, the night staff, would be there. One evening she fell into Greg's arms, sobbing. Carly handed her two beers and sent her on her way. She was scared but she knew if there was anything she needed, she could call, and they would help. These people were angels, sent to her each day to remind her she was not alone. They were watching over her.

There was the valet who took good care of her car, and each morning and night gave Justice a treat. He made sure she got what she needed and even offered a bottle of wine now and then.

There were the girls at the front desk. Lovingly talking to her as her girlfriends did. They were moms and wives, too, and could relate to her and how her life was flipped around. They knew she was trying to balance her caregiver role and mother to Katherine and Peter. They put themselves in her shoes and offered understanding of what happens to a family when a husband is sick. The fear of a wife and mother they could understand. They offered their shoulders to lean on, each and every day. She was so grateful for their love and support each morning and every night.

The people at the breakfast bar offered a warm "Good Morning" greeting. They were cheerful, and the coffee was delicious! They gave hugs and comfort, as well as positive vibes each day.

The housekeepers were extra careful, always making sure when the kids came there were extra linens and towels. Humble and quiet, they did their job knowing the hurt she was feeling. But they always smiled and greeted her warmly.

The staff seemed to know exactly what she needed and when. They could see it in her puffy eyes when she had spent the day crying. Sometimes she confided in them more than her family and friends. They were there and witnessed daily the grief and stress she was experiencing. They saw her at her most vulnerable. She appreciated being able to open up to them.

They, Peg and the staff, were a family of caring individuals from different backgrounds and places. People she never thought would be her friends became her friends. These people were pillars of strength. Angels sent from heaven to watch out for her at the right time.

She will forever be grateful to these individuals who were there day in and day out, morning, noon, and night to provide love, comfort, and support as she and her family healed together.

Due to never feeling isolated or alone, Peg was able to draw strength and courage from these people while she stayed at her "hotel home." She looks back now and wonders where these people live, what kind of family they are from, and more. But while she lived in the hotel, they became her family.

BEHIND THE SCENES...LOVE

As Peg navigated her days, she was also tuning out life around her. The world was going on, world events were moving forward, New England won the super bowl, etc., etc. Life back home continued to move forward, too. Their kids were living on their own yet had the full support of the family surrounding them.

And soon Peg and Rick would be going back to a home they called "summer home." This was not what they had signed up for. Pointe Verde is quiet in the off season. Family and friends go back to their busy lives. Lights go out and days become shorter and shorter. How was she to manage this while staying positive and realistic at the same time?

The beach house was under construction; it was a complete mess! Katherine and Peter were dealing with everything. This meant putting ramps at the front and back entrance so Rick's wheelchair could enter and exit the house. It meant converting a bedroom and bath into what looked like a hospital room with handicap bars everywhere and a hospital bed. Rick slept in that bed for months while Peg slept on the sofa in order to be close to him. The renovation was not a pretty project—it was ugly! Carolyn, Brenda, and Grady, Rick's cousins, were spearheading the project, helping the kids along the way. They would be there to make sure the house was finished to the last detail.

They also helped Peg pack up the apartment in Port St. Louis. They came in and got the job done. This is who they were. When needed, they showed up without questions or fuss.

As Peg prepared to bring her husband home she began to panic, realizing the challenges that lay ahead. But she never had anything to worry about as family and friends were there for her. Dinners were being planned for their arrival home, the house being renovated, flowers being planted, and groceries being delivered. Everyone was doing their part to make the transition home as smooth as possible. Grateful, so grateful she was, for arriving home not having to worry about these things. Even as their lives were forever changed, the constant support of family and friends remained the same. Knowing that life was changed forever, Peg prayed each day that God would continue to give her strength to keep her family and home safe and secure.

As the wheelchair van drove away from the safety of rehab, Peg stared out the window and cried. She looked at Rick strapped in the wheelchair and prayed for HOPE. Just then the theme song from *Love Story,* their favorite movie, began to play on the radio.

SLOWLY, THE HEALING BEGAN

Rick continued to get stronger; slowly laughter and emotion started to come back. Glimmers of JOY were shining through each day. His determination and will to be better was stronger each day.

Their angels appeared to help offer strength and guidance. The aides appeared around the clock. Strangers who became invisible angels, offering signs and giving Rick more of himself back. Having strangers in her house became normal. Just another part of the healing process for her family. Total strangers once again giving more strength than ever could be imagined.

Days with Rick were quiet. He was quiet but always began the day with, "I love you," and ended the day with, "I love you." Peg admired his ability to find glimmers of joy in the simple things that life brings—a walk on the beach, looking at a sunset, sharing a great meal, reading a good book, watching a romantic movie, being with the kids, and laughing. It's the simplest things in life that bring the most JOY.

Rick and Peg made it back to their favorite restaurant on Pointe Verde. Months earlier, while sitting with the kids, she had said to the owner, "My goal is to get Rick here by the end of summer." And there they were! It was quite an accomplishment, one that Peg was so proud of.

Peg sat there, sipping a glass of wine and looking at her family. "Rick, make a toast," and he said, "To the four of us, and all the happiness we will have." With tears in their eyes, they clinked glasses. They were ready to make new memories together. There were smiles and laughs all around that night as they discussed a new addition to the family. Baby Brady, a new puppy, was on the way!!

Manifest, and it will happen, no matter what. If you truly believe and want something, it will happen. Treasure each day and make it count…keep those you love close…always say I love you…always share a hug goodbye because you never know when or where you will see each other again.

On New Year's Eve, Peg quietly let go of 2017, and the hardship and disappointments that had been part of it and welcomed the blessings the new year would bring. In bed at 10:00 pm, Peg thought to herself that it was a time of truly practicing what she had been taught. Live in the present moment, as if it were the last.

"Treasure the smiles, good times, and memories and leave behind the disappointments, hard times, and enemies. Hold onto faith, hope and beliefs, and may the new year be filled with love, joy, and peace."
                                                              ~ Author unknown

The quote above was sent to me by a friend. It inspired me, and reminded me of the important things in life.

Chapter 13

♥

FINDING JOY IN THE JOURNEY

"Finding joy in the journey." What does this mean?? As Peg drove to yoga class she thought about her life and where it was going. She was thinking of her novel that was sitting there waiting to be finished. She was thinking of asking the studio owner to put her back on the sub list and about teaching again. The question on Peg's mind was how to get back to the life she loved and the things she loved to do? Her time had been so consumed with Rick's needs and making sure the kids were okay that she had let go of *her* dreams.

The yoga class was packed, and it was 100 degrees out. She almost did not go in. Although she loved the energy of the packed classes, she was in the mood for a little more space. It was noisy in the studio, and she tried to quiet her mind. Setting the intention of acceptance. The class began and her body moved and soon sweat was dripping down her face.

Peg welcomed the quietness of shavasana "corpse" pose, being completely still with her breath. As the class ended in one single OM, the universe was ready to speak to her once again. "The light in me honors the divine light in you...Namaste."

Peg looked up and there she was—this beautiful soul she met two years prior while in training. Ann and Peg immediately hugged and reconnected. Ann was a meditation teacher and was planning to open her own yoga studio. As they caught up on life, Peg filled Ann in on Rick's accident and how their world had been flipped upside down. She immediately said, "You both need a meditation practice.

You need this to heal his brain and your hearts. Also, would you want to come and teach at my studio?" Here was her gift, her sign from the universe saying, "It's time, it's your time."

"YES, I would love to!"

"Good, I will add the class to our schedule. So glad you will be a part of my team!"

Overwhelmed with excitement, Peg could hardly wait to get home and tell Rick about her teaching opportunity and ask him about doing meditation together. He, as usual, was so supportive and onboard with what became known as "meditation Mondays." This was their first step as the new Peg and Rick. New adventures, activities to do together, other than PT!

The next day Peg and Rick drove to a park where they began a biking program. This was so exciting! They rode the beautiful and peaceful trail for 3.2 miles! Rick got on and off the bike with help from the therapist while feeling alive and free. Rick was exhausted and slept in the afternoon. Peg was smiling ear to ear thinking that she and her husband did this fun activity together! She felt like they were a couple once again.

LIFE IS ALWAYS CHANGING

Peg wanted it to be a perfect day of celebrating. Out of the corner of her eye she saw Rick, but she could not get there fast enough. He was getting up and his body was off balance. He fell hard. Peg ran over, falling on the floor with him. He was unable to move his leg. WTF? How could this be happening again? How could she be in the front seat of an ambulance on her way to another emergency room? This could not be happening! Her entire being was numb.

As she heard the words from the doctor, she felt like puking. "I am sorry, but the x-ray shows a broken hip. We are looking at a hip replacement." This meant weeks or months of rehab. They had worked so hard the entire year and now to have this major setback they never saw coming. Back to surgery, back to rehab, back on a walker. Really, this was complete bullshit!! Once again everything was taken from them. All the progress was stripped away! Why? She was not supposed to ask why, just to trust the process. Well, that was hard to do!! She called her sister-in-law who came to the hospital. They stayed with Rick until 2:00 am. Peg arrived home to her son making dinner for her. He made her eat before she cried herself to sleep.

She called each of her dear friends and her sister to help her through another crisis. To help her stay strong and steady. These friends would be with her once again.

The next day Rick had the operation. Katherine and Peter showed up. This event brought them closer. Their relationship was shifting but the universe aligned them once again, and they leaned on each other. Since Rick had come home from rehab the kids went about their days and the conversations in the house were less and less. They came into the pre-op room with a look of fear Peg had not seen since they left the ICU, a fear of losing their dad. "This can be fixed," she had told them the night before. "It is a hip replacement, not another brain injury!" Everyone was silent. Peg knew she had to hold strong and guide her family once again through a difficult period. She had to keep them safe and whole.

As Rick was rolled away, the three of them walked in silence to the waiting area. Peg hugged them both. She did not want them to have to spend hours in the hospital, so she told them to take care of each other and sent them out into the pouring rain, saying a little prayer to her earthly father in heaven.

"Dad, watch over Katherine and Peter. Let them know they are loved and safe, be with them always."

Just then her phone buzzed. It was Patsy, a friend who often phoned whenever she was thinking about her dad. "Who is with you?" Patsy asked. "My dad," Peg answered.

She received so many messages from the universe, from God, and from her dad. This was another sure sign that her father was with her, listening to her, and certainly watching out for their kids.

Peg sat alone in the waiting room for three hours. Praying, waiting, praying more, and waiting. For hope and peace for her family.

As she waited, her best friend Jill called, "I am on my way, no questions asked!" Peg felt relief to know she would not be alone much longer. Girlfriends are so important, and friendships can be near or far. As she navigated her way through life, this became clearer and clearer. Never losing sight of these friends who lifted her up.

The operation was a success! Now it was time to go to rehab and recover, but not only for Rick. She knew what had to be done to heal herself, too. Sometimes you have to loosen your grip. She was reminded of this once again. Let God handle it. There is no point in trying to control what can or may happen in life, especially on this journey.

Rick stayed in rehab for three weeks. This time she backed off a bit and let him take charge of the situation. She invited his family and friends to help, welcoming the break. There were some feelings of guilt, but it was a much-needed break, not only for her, but the kids as well. No aides in the house, no worry about accidents happening, no worry about medications and daily care, wheeling chairs in, etc. They had freedom again, for a short bit. Rick needed to be where he was to get stronger and clearer about his next steps, and how he wanted to show up in his life from now on.

He did get better and strong enough to come home again. The first day back was the hardest. Peg watched him as another caretaker came in the door. She left and drove away, not wanting to go back. The feeling was overwhelming and suffocating. She was afraid that this is what her life would be, so she kept driving. She stopped for coffee and cried. She called Jill who tried to talk her through it. She met Rick's sister, Kim, and crumbled in her arms. Kim was her "Pointe Verde Sista'." Peg adored Kim, and her strength. They walked for over an hour. At last Peg was able to take a deep breath and walk back into her house, into this "new normal." Healing comes in all shapes and sizes. The good, bad, ugly, and uglier. There is no right or wrong way to do it. But one thing is for sure, you have to take care of yourself in order to hold space for the ones you love.

Peg's friends and family gave her the strength she needed to move forward. Whatever was going to unfold was not in her control, and she had to accept that at all costs.

FRIENDSHIPS

"Look at these folks as expanders in your life…instead of holding sadness and resentment…know that they are holding space for you. They are showing you life can go on…maybe slower, maybe different, but it can go on and the laughter and smiles will return."
                              ~ Quote from Peg's spiritual coach and dear friend.

As the months passed, various friends would come in and out of Peg's life. She would push herself to meet new people since she was alone on Pointe Verde, and she would rely on old friends to call for comfort and love. She remembers telling her daughter after a visit from her friends, "Always stay close to your girlfriends. They will be there for you no matter what, travel far to comfort you, and offer you strength when you are feeling alone." This would hold true for Peg. She was learning that to be happy it was up to her to find her true happiness and to do things that filled her cup with love and joy. She would have to leave Rick behind at times, to be with her friends, both new and old, to find the happiness in her life.

So many friends, even some family members, were uncomfortable with Peg and Rick's new situation and the changes in their lives. When there is a mess, sometimes people simply do not want to deal with it. The hurt was strong, but she understood and let it go. Their "couple" friends remained constant for the most part. There were a few that drifted away, but that was okay.

Hanging onto resentment and anger was not part of her life. She would no longer use that energy because it drained her. Instead, she leaned on those who truly cared. The friends that fed her soul. The ones that lifted her up and the couples who lifted her and Rick up.

When Rick broke his hip, Peg felt like a little girl once again—alone and scared to death. The girl left at the train station who needed a ride, the girl who needed the strength of her girlfriends to push through this storm.

These friends knew Peg before she became a wife and mother. They knew her insecurities, her deepest fears, and they showed up to help her through this.

JILL

Peg and Jill walked for hours along the beach, sometimes talking, sometimes silent, noticing the nature around them. Jill was in awe of the baby birds hatching and the ocean itself. They talked about how Peg needed to heal, how she needed relationships to shift in her own life, and that she needed her independence to find JOY in her life. Jill told her, "Rick needs to feel empowered and independent. He needs to own this recovery. You need to back away a little. Be there for support, but do not get consumed in his recovery! It is time for you to recover now!"

The walk ended with a beautiful breakfast at an inn on the waterfront. It was exactly what Peg needed and where she needed to be. Peg said a prayer of thanks and knew all was going to be okay in time. Being by the sea with her friend and soaking it all in was a time she is truly grateful for.

CLAIRE

Peg's friendships are amazing and solid. When Rick was in ICU her friends came and sat with her, called her, and cooked for her. Claire came from out of state without a word, made a beautiful dinner, and walked the dog without even being asked. She simply showed up and found a way into the apartment. When Peg was alone late at night, her friends would call, and she would cry for hours with them. Peg drew strength from each one of them.

Claire, nurturing and always so positive, left her inspirational messages every morning so she could begin her day with a positive meditation. She was there at the drop of a dime, no matter what. She sent notes and gifts to the kids at college, helping to keep their spirits high and positive. This woman was a true angel from heaven.

Peg and Claire met while in college. Claire was a bit of a wild child. They knew each other through parties and sometimes hung out in a larger group but were never really connected. Finals week arrived, and it was Peg's birthday. Peg was done with her final exams, but no one could go out to celebrate due to having to study for finals. Claire knocked on Peg's door and the two of them ventured to the local bar for $0.25 Happy Hour. They drank gin and tonic all night and from there became the best of friends. Bonding instantly and sharing so much. Over the years they were in each other's weddings, and they welcomed children into the world. During Peg's infertility it was Claire who comforted her. She was a selfless soul. Always doing and helping others. Working six days a week and volunteering in shelters on the seventh. Authentic in every aspect. Showing up with LOVE wherever she went and helping people was her true nature. She did it quietly and wanted absolutely no recognition. Peg was beyond grateful for the night they spent in the bar drinking gin. Without that evening, she would not have met this amazing woman she now calls her best friend.

When Claire decided to move to Florida several months after Rick's accident it was bittersweet. Even though they saw each other only a few times a year, the thought of Claire being a three-hour plane ride away frightened Peg. Not the fear of flying, but that her best friend who had always been there for her would now be so far away and unable to come quickly when Peg needed her. But Claire had to make this big move for her own well-being and Peg would be supportive, as always. In the days before her move, Peg and Claire spent time on

Pointe Verde. A day spent in Southport with Claire and her friend Charlotte was the BEST day of that long summer of change.

As they pulled into Southport Harbor, Peg felt as if she were on a different planet. The heaviness of stress and worry lifted. She shut her phone off and spent the day in the moment. Strolling the cobblestone streets, finding her favorite stores, and enjoying a glass of champagne and halibut salad on the beach at her favorite restaurant. Talking for hours, laughing, and crying with these amazing women who filled her soul with strength and love. It was a day imprinted in her memory forever. A day of true beauty in every aspect. Not a cloud in the sky; the ocean as blue and as calm as could be in the presence of forever friends.

Peg cried while saying goodbye to Claire and Charlotte. Scared to go back to life as it was, but knowing she was much safer and stronger. The old Peg was gone, the old Rick was gone, and she was ready to embrace their life as it was now, continuing to find joy in each day.

PATSY

Patsy brought messages from the Lord. She constantly reminded Peg that God was right there beside her and watching over her family. She was a light of laughter. She was the one who gave Peg a shoe on the streets of Burlington and told her to throw it against the building and shout and cry as loud as she could. Patsy would be there for her when she was sobbing and needed a clear message from God. She was a constant reminder that it was okay not to be okay. They were distant friends, but Patsy showed up stronger than ever for Peg at this time in her life. She wrapped her arms around Peg and gave her God's will to carry on. Peg's faith grew due to her connection with Patsy. Peg now went to mass and listened not to the priests but the quiet messages from the Lord and His Mother Mary that would come through loud and clear. She was paying attention to her faith and learning more about it. She was able to calm herself knowing the Lord was with her and she was never alone.

CHARLOTTE

Charlotte helped in the wee hours of the night. Peg called her asking for clear advice on all the logistics that needed to be done. She was the one who gave Peg the courage to advocate for herself and for Rick. The courage to insist on the help and support needed in order to get Rick safely home. She was the one Peg relied on to confirm everything was okay and to encourage her to always stand up for herself.

TAMARIN

Tamarin was always so positive and strong, calm and caring. She sat with Peg at the hospital on a very long day to offer support and comfort.

FLO

Flo prayed and prayed and prayed and used her humor to brighten the dark days.

DAN AND BARBARA

Dan and Barbara, two of their closest friends, were friends for life. Even though life was different, these two friends stayed right by their side. Including them in dinners, visiting, and offering help and support in so many ways. Yes, it was awkward at times, but their friendship overcame that, and they understood what Peg and Rick were going through. Peg did not have to put on airs with them. Dan and Rick have been the best of friends for years, and this friendship came through even in the most difficult of times.

STEVE AND GISELE

Peg remembers the day Steve and Gisele, who were also a constant in their lives, came to visit and lunch on the Pointe Verde canal. The day was filled with laughter and love. It was a perfect day, and the water was so calm, just like the calm Peg was feeling at that time. Steve and Gisele came every few months to visit. The first visit was shaky, as Rick was in a wheelchair, and everyone was left in tears. But after the lunch visit on the canal, they all left laughing, even Rick. It was a sure sign of healing.

SISTERS-IN-LAW AND SISTERS

Peg will always call her dear sisters-in-law her SISTERS. Marta spent late nights with her watching Rick struggle for his life and holding onto Peg when she fell apart. Laura brought food to them every weekend in the trauma unit. Kim brought her to the most beautiful church and sat by her side and prayed. Angela drove miles to Peter's college to watch him play lacrosse and brought food for his teammates.

Peg's own sister was the friend she absolutely confided everything to. She told Sara she needed Rick to have his mind back. She told her how terrified she was that he would not come back to them. Sara held her and listened. She was her confidante and had her back no matter what had to be done.

BROTHERS-IN-LAW

Her brother-in-law, Mark, was there in every way for her family. He silently sat back and knew what had to be done to ensure his niece and nephew felt completely safe and secure. He was there for their kids whenever they needed him.

Her brother-in-law, Sam, was with her during the darkest of moments when Rick was realizing what was happening to his life. He stayed by his brother's side offering support and strength.

RICK'S WORK AND FRIENDS

Losing his job was devastating for Rick. His entire life was his work and the relationships he built there over thirty-four years. These were not just work colleagues, they were his friends. Peg began to understand this as life went on and she formed her own relationships with these people.

Jan, Rick's co-worker and a member of his sales team, would often visit and fill Rick in on everything happening at work, making him feel included in something he had cherished for so long.

Jan organized a dinner, a night of laughing and joking in which her husband owned the conversation for the first time in almost two years. Rick sat tall at the head of the table, making eye contact, and joking about his hair gel, busting chops, and really enjoying the company. These friends did not look at Rick differently; their friend was here, and these friendships were forever.

While dealing with the changes in their own relationship it was hard for Peg to handle changes with friends too. For example, running into a couple at the beach while walking their dogs on their wedding anniversary. To Peg they seemed carefree and happy, running and hugging each other. Laughing and telling her they would call. After this encounter, Peg sat in the car with tears rolling down her cheeks. She felt she and Rick could no longer do what this couple were doing and wondered if they would ever be that carefree again.

FINDING LIFE AGAIN

What does finding life again mean? A new normal, a new day, taking it day by day—who knows? All she knew was that it was time to take care of herself, to heal herself so her husband could continue healing and their kids could heal. Taking care of herself had to become front and center in order for her to care for everyone else. Her body was screaming at her, her eczema was in overdrive. She had ignored it for months. Her heart was breaking, and she had to fix it; her mind was out of control. Every day was the same, and she was putting out fires everywhere. All this had to be addressed, but how?

Chapter 14

SELF-CARE

It seems so simple. Go get a massage and be done with it, one may think. It is *so* much more than that! What did it mean for Peg, and how could she take care of herself in ways that would help her heal while still allowing her to be there for Rick? Self-care for Peg came in many forms.

She started a consecutive mediation practice to allow her mind to be quiet, so her subconscious thoughts could rise to the surface. She started to do things that fulfilled her. Walks on the beach, sitting on the beach, doing yoga, meeting girlfriends for lunch and coffee, reading books, eating good foods, planting flowers, writing, teaching yoga, and decorating her home. All this slowly gave Peg a sense of herself.

Working with a Spiritual trauma coach and therapist, Peg learned how to incorporate practices in times of stress. She noticed triggers in her life. She looked for the right people to help her navigate through the change and trauma.

She also dove back into her book, slowly creating her novel that she wanted to share so much. She stopped caring what other people thought of her. If they were interested, great, if not, so be it. She stopped trying to be someone she was not. For many years she had always wanted to please others and molded herself to be the person she thought would fit in. She was beginning to see herself for who she was, not who others thought she was. Peg was on her way back to her authentic self.

Each day she found more joy in each moment…the small things made her happy again. Sitting quietly by the fire, cooking meals, and spending time with her kids. Watching a sunset or staring at the ocean. It was in these moments she felt spirit. She felt a light of love. And that was just what Peg needed at that time in her life.

For when we sit in these moments, our own light shines and our mind is clear. It is in moments of quiet that we understand the next steps. That's when we trust that the universe is sending us exactly what is needed to face each moment that comes. When we sit with any discomfort we are facing, whether it is a situation, a person, or whatever, big or small, we find we can sit there and ride the wave of discomfort. These were the times Peg knew she would be okay with whatever was to be for her life, her family's life, and her marriage.

As Peg began to find these truths, she also found herself distancing from people who did not understand her change. Many people wanted Rick and Peg's life to look like it had two years prior. This caused some people to stop coming around, or simply kept conversations light. Previously Peg would have gotten upset when this happened. But with time, she came to understand that she was pulling away. Making a conscious effort not to be around people or situations that did not serve her higher being. Avoiding situations which brought discomfort and unease into her life. She would rather keep close the ones who brought encouragement, good words, and pure love.

As she dove deeper and deeper into this work of self-care and self-nurture, she began to feel a sense of her truth coming back. She was not going to let this accident define her or her family. She was beginning to understand that this did not happen "to" them but happened "for" them. She decided to live her life like this, finding every chance she possibly could to be thankful and truly grateful for something, no matter how the day was going. Deciding before she went to bed that the day ahead was going to be wonderful, no matter what. This meant paying attention to life. Not defending who she was or what she was doing. Changing slowly and not caring how that looked to anyone but herself. Following the path, and trusting she was about to launch something big.

Waking each morning, she sat in meditation, not forcing anything and allowing the universe to speak through her. Allowing whatever it was she was supposed to do to rise to the surface. Her thoughts were quiet but not silenced, and she was able to face each new day with a higher sense of purpose.

Who am I? What do I want? What is my purpose? What am I grateful for?

These were the four questions she put out to the universe, not answering but allowing herself to subconsciously see what happened. A shift began, and slowly she understood.

Change

"You never have to defend anything you are doing," her trauma and spiritual coach told her. So very true! After working on her own self-care practice, Peg began to understand that she had to bring in everything that served her higher vibration, and she had to be around people who lifted her up and held her safe. This all meant accepting change, accepting that relationships change, and that it was all okay. It was okay to decline invitations, it was okay to distance yourself from friends, and even family members. It was all okay because self-care was about taking care of Peg so she could properly take care of Rick, Katherine, and Peter, the family she cherished.

Rick's last days of therapy were scary, for sure. He was discharged and sent off on his own. Not knowing how it would be, he trusted his therapist to get him to the point that he could go out and LIVE!! He was walking on his own using a cane, using his right arm a small amount, and thinking clearly again. His brain was healing, a mystery no one could explain! It was time and Rick and Peg both knew it. After almost two years in hospitals and rehab, it was time to be on their own.

Text Message To Katherine And Peter

"Well, we made it! Dad was discharged from all his therapies today. This is a GOOD thing. Now it is time to live life! The doctor wants dad to walk and challenge himself as much as possible. Continue to work daily on cognitive puzzles, reading, playing games, and doing all his exercises daily. Laugh, love, and enjoy his life while setting goals for himself. His brain continues to heal. Dad is on board with all of this and has made a commitment to continue all his hard work in order to get stronger and stronger. This has been a journey, and I am beyond proud of Dad. Inside and out, he has fought so hard, never giving up for one second and never complaining. We all live life now—not taking one minute for granted. Love has healed our family and has gotten us to this point. This accident does not define Dad or our family. It did not happen "to" us, but it happened "for" us. Why? We are not allowed to ask, but someday the answer will be clear, I just know it!!

Thank you for your LOVE, support, and comfort. Go live life for your father who adores each of you so much! Might be slowed down a little, but it gives us time to smell the roses!!

I LOVE you.
Mom"

Peg pressed the send button on her phone; she knew this was the most important message to send to their kids who needed to know life was okay, love healed, and that each minute, each breath is a gift. And, most importantly, to live each day with a purpose.

We Made It!

Having settled in at Gret's Rock, their house completed and finally feeling somewhat like home, Peg started to form some routines and practices she and Rick could live by.

For their Monday meditations, no place was more perfect than the studio in town. It was bright and beautiful, very low key, and the owner was a bright, shining light. The first time was scary for both of them, but Josie made them feel at ease and her warm energy surrounded them. "This did not happen to you…it happened for you!" Josie reminded them. They now knew not to be defined by this accident. They found joy in those moments of quiet.

Peg and Rick had always planned to retire in Florida; keeping that plan was important to them. They were looking forward to Florida, and the warmth was needed for continued healing. As they were preparing to leave Pointe Verde so much had to be done. How would she manage? Amazingly, she did not find it overwhelming. Staying present brought her the peace and time she needed to do this. Another big move in their lives. But she trusted Rick (and this time herself, too) completely in that this was what was needed to continue their healing together as a couple. They needed to regroup and continue to find love.

Their last night of meditation before leaving, they said their goodbyes to strangers who had become dear friends and headed to their favorite inn on the waterfront. It was Christmas time, and the lights were spectacular. They walked silently, arm in arm through the lobby, no fear of falling, no more wheelchair or gate belts. They were slow but this gave them time to appreciate the surroundings.

The lobby was grand; the Christmas tree was huge and spectacular, and a beautiful gingerbread house took up half the lobby. Peg stopped and looked around. They were the only two in the lobby, as if the universe was saying—stop, don't rush, breathe it all in. She took a photo of Rick staring at the tree and soaked in his expression of gratitude. She walked towards him; he reached out, pulled her close, and hugged her tightly with both strong arms. Peg felt safe again. She felt secure, loved, and comforted. His strong scent was present. Tears rolled down both their cheeks. They journeyed back to each other. They had a delicious dinner in the cozy bar. Basking in the love they had for the life they were looking forward to, and the excitement of a new chapter in their lives.

THE OCEAN

It was so cold that morning, but the sun was finally out and there was not a cloud in the sky. Peg got up at 5:30 am, as usual, and meditated. Her daily mantra was love and kindness. Afterwards she sat quietly by the fire. One week from now they would be in Florida, staying for four months. She had mixed feelings but was trusting this was the right move.

She went to yoga and her teacher reminded her to prepare for changes and to let go of control. Peg knew that in life we have no control, especially concerning people and situations that simply do not want to change. And this is what she focused on.

After class she found herself by the sea. The blues of the sea and sky contrasting with one another were amazing. Peg took it all in. She walked by the water. She walked and walked and walked. There was not one thought on her mind, and all was still and quiet. She did not think of the day ahead, her husband, her kids, her mom, the "to do" list. The only sound she heard was that of the waves...waves that carried her through the storm.

Did this mean she was finally free of control, hurt, sadness, and guilt? She continued walking with spirit, praying for love and kindness. Peg was ready for change, ready to close this chapter and put worry away. She had no idea what lay ahead, but knew she had to stay present and find JOY in the journey.

Chapter 15

Moving to Florida, Winter 2019

Driving to the airport in Burlington, they were both quiet. As they crossed the bridge, Peg said a prayer for peace. The ride seemed to take forever. The silence was so thick. They were both deep in thought about what lay ahead. Going to a home they had not seen, building a life far away from Gret's Rock, and being far away from their kids. So many emotions. The plane ride was uneventful, and they landed safe and sound. Peg said another prayer for peace.

As soon as the warmth hit them, it was as though they both woke up from a fog. They smiled at each other, and Rick said, "This is it!" Thus, they entered a new chapter, a new life together. Always moving forward.

The first day was hectic. Rick's entire family was there to help with the transition, and it was a blessing having so many hands. One by one they left to go back to their lives and Peg felt more and more alone. It was scary. The house would be quiet again and she would have to figure out how to manage all this on her own in a strange place. Katherine and Peter went back to their lives too, as they should. Rick's siblings left knowing he was okay…but was Peg? The fear of being alone was overwhelming. The fear of something happening kept her up at night. It was time to re-group!

First things first! She found a yoga studio and landed on her mat. Listening to the same mantra that tore her apart and put her back together. She inhaled deeply, exhaled, and knew she would be okay. She knew in her heart they were going to find their way again, find where they fit in, and figure out what to do. Through yoga, as usual, she met people and eventually felt at home. Once again, thanks to yoga, she found her space, her sacred space anytime she wanted.

The studio was all about love, and that had been her mantra; love and kindness, love and patience. It was welcoming and small; it was spiritual and comforting. She felt it the minute she walked in the door; this was the right yoga studio for her to continue on her path toward healing. As she went deeper into child pose, the tears flowed. She knew she had found her way home. She knew in her heart that her family would be whole again.

Yoga once again became so important. Meditating each day helped Peg dig deep inside to discover what she truly wanted, what her purpose was, and where the joy would come from.

Some days she had no idea how she would do it—but every day it was done. Life goes on, and the sun always comes up.

Peg and Rick found a "new love"—and it was all okay.

Who am I … LOVE

What do I want … LOVE

What is my purpose … LOVE

What am I grateful for … LOVE

Peg's mom passed away that winter, while Peg was away. Peg had not seen her mom in almost two years, since Rick's accident. Her mom had not been able to leave the house due to her health issues. She had also never gotten over the loss of her husband. She went to a dark place where Peg was petrified to go. Peg knew she could not allow her mother to take her there, to a place of sadness, hurt, and emotional fear. So Peg stayed away and did not call as often.

Their relationship had been fragile, but her mom had always been just a phone call away. The night before she died, they had a great conversation and as always it ended with, "I love you, take care of yourself." Peg will remember that last conversation and those words even as she continues to heal and find her own soul.

When Peg heard the news of her mom's passing, she felt sad. But there was also a sense of peace. Knowing her mother was free of fear, pain, and loss of emotional control was comforting. Instead of mourning her mother's death, Peg celebrated her life by remembering the good times and the good conversations with her mother.

The celebration of mass was on Mother's Day weekend, the day after Peg's birthday. The night before, Rick had planned a beautiful dinner with the kids and her sisters' families. They laughed and cried, and it was an amazing time. The service was in the chapel within the cathedral. It was a small, intimate space. The lilacs were in full bloom, and she could smell their fragrance as she entered the space. The Blessed Mother greeted them at the entrance, the most beautiful representation Peg had ever seen. They were then greeted by the Priest. Peg watched as everyone came up for communion and knew that each person was supposed to be there. They were the final angels; they were there to take her mother to heaven and to give Peg the peace she needed to move forward.

Rick held her that day in a way he had not done in two years. His strength was there for her. He walked out of the church with her, slow and brave, ready, and confident. Peg felt a glimpse of the Rick she always leaned on, trusted, and depended on to be there in times of crisis.

After the burial, Peg, Rick, Peter, and Katherine went to lunch. They loved being together and eating good food, and they did it well. Peg laughed with the kids and told them how very proud she was of them.

"I am the luckiest mom alive today. To have had both of you brought from across the world to me! I love you; I adore you!! On Mother's Day I always pray for your birth mothers who gave you life and chose to give you to me. You do the same. We have weathered a storm together, the

three of us, and brought our family through…it could not have happened without both of you by my side!"

They then said their good-byes and went on with their lives. Peg would long for Memorial Day weekend when they would all be together again.

Chapter 16

RED LIPSTICK PEG

Twenty years ago, Peg worked at a shoe company, she led a nationwide team of 600 managers. Twenty years ago, she only wore red lipstick and red nail polish. Twenty years ago, she was carefree, a little wild, and laughed all the time. Twenty years ago, she did not have to have a clean, perfect house, a groomed yard, and everything in its place. When did things start to change? Over the years she had tried to fit in by dressing a certain way, acting a certain way, not speaking her truth, losing independence, and being told what to do. Now, she sits with two friends who knew her twenty years ago at that shoe company and they are asking her what happened to her red lipstick and red nails? These women remind her of her true self. She had to be brave enough to come undone, to fall, and to be vulnerable in order to be that girl she had been. The girl she loved and adored, the one who only wore red lipstick. The one who had been brave enough to step back. Brave enough TO LAUGH AND LOVE AND SAY WHATEVER WAS ON HER MIND. To be able to DECLINE INVITATIONS, TO CHANGE UP FRIENDSHIPS AND ROUTINES, TO BE WITH PEOPLE WHO LIFTED HER SPIRITS, TO BE BRAVE ENOUGH TO BE COMPLETELY AUTHENTIC. This is where her true work would begin!

Chapter 17

Planting And Nature. Pointe Verde, Summer 2019

She had to begin somewhere, so what better place than Mother Earth where all healing takes place. Walking around the nursery with her cousin, touching plants and smelling flowers and herbs was the most amazing mindful meditation she had experienced in a long time. She and her cousin talked about their mothers; two sisters. In doing so they brought these two women together again. And together they found joy and strength.

Peg turned to her cousin and said, "You know, being with nature is the best way to heal and de-stress." They spent the day in Peg's yard at Gret's Rock, turning it into a beautiful sanctuary of color, flowers, and herbs. With love, her yard came back to life just as her life was slowly doing. The energy she felt in the yard was infectious. She knew from that point on, only positive energy was to come into all spaces in her life. She began, little by little, transforming her home, making each and every room into a place of comfort, love, and support. She longed for good energy everywhere.

Peg woke at 5:30 am and did her morning meditation. She lit her candle and sat very still. Birds were waking and the sounds of nature were all around her. The kids were both asleep, Rick was asleep, the dogs were sleeping. Everything was still and safe. The people she adored were there and safe. It was a sense of calm and peace. She dwelled in this space knowing all too well that storms come to shake things up.

But how to manage it all, without falling off the edge or drowning in fear, was her job. Sometimes constant fear engulfed her and learning to let it go and put safety measures in place was the next step toward healing. Rick longs for his meditation times as well. He, too, is finding a way to calm the fears he feels now that he is on this new path.

They both support each other in ways no one can imagine. They look around at their new life, this new way of being with LOVE, hope, and knowing. Healing is taking place and they *are* growing from this place of peace. Trying not to worry about the future and finding quiet moments of complete gratitude for the life they have. Not worrying about what they are missing or do not have, but instead doing things that fill their hearts with LOVE and JOY. Peg is committed to her practices and will help Rick along the way.

If they were not driving around in convertibles, beaching every day, drinking with friends, boating, golfing, going to cocktail parties, or traveling the country, they would learn to be quiet. The stillness and reality of life was settling in. They were processing, wondering what to do with these days and nights as their friends and family continued with their busy lives. They found themselves doing things they never would have done together. They found meditation, music, shows to watch, and new restaurants to try for lunch. They found themselves watching sunsets together, getting up early to enjoy quiet mornings, and realizing and accepting what they could share with friends and what they no longer could give to these people.

Patsy and her husband flew into town. Patsy brought good energy. They laughed, cried, and sang. Her husband played guitar. Peg picked up the guitar she used to play, and it felt good—it was at that moment she realized she had lost herself somewhere along the way. She lost part of the spirit. The spirit Rick fell in love with. She tried to fit in and do what she was supposed to do. To dress the part of the preppy wife when in fact she was a free spirit. She loved funky jewelry, red lipstick, and colorful clothing. Wild hair, dancing, singing, music, and laughter. As she held that guitar, she knew she needed to find her spirit again. She needed to surround herself with people who lifted her vibration and made her feel whole and loved. To continue to heal her family, she needed to heal herself, by bringing back that free spirit. Get back to that girl who was light and who loved fun and was loving, authentic, and kind. Find her—BE HER!!

Peg was determined to find her former self and to live authentically as her true spirit. She knew that yoga and meditation would play a big part in doing this. These things would bring her back to her red lipstick, carefree, wild hair days.

Peg had learned in yoga that as you grow in self-awareness, you remove the blocks to your full potential and naturally live in tune with your true purpose. She had also learned how meditation played an important role in this process.

Peg's meditation instructor had taught her that before beginning any meditation session, she should ask herself the four questions:

Who truly am I? What do I truly want? What am I truly grateful for? What is my dharma or purpose in life?

It doesn't matter if answers don't come immediately. Simply ask the questions and let them go as you enter the inner quiet of meditation.

Who truly am I?

What do I truly want?

What am I truly grateful for?

What is my dharma or purpose in life?

As Peg reflected and meditated on the four questions, it became clear how she should navigate and manage this new life. Life starts out as pure LOVE. That is why we need to believe that with LOVE all is healed, all is good, all is the way it should be.

Who truly am I?

Peg sat with this question for a long time, months actually. She was a daughter, a wife, a mother, a friend, a yoga instructor, a writer, a golfer, etc.

Who truly am I…LOVE!

What do I truly want?

Good health for my family, success for the kids, strength each day for Rick, etc.

What do I truly want…LOVE!

What really is my purpose?

Peg sat for months on this one as well. To care for my family, take care of Rick and the kids, help Rick back to life, write a book, be a good friend, etc.

What really is my purpose…LOVE

What am I truly grateful for?

My family, recovery, Rick's healing, our life, friends, and family.

What am I truly grateful for…LOVE

Each question, little by little, became so clear—months of meditation brought Peg to the point of realizing, it was LOVE all along. The love she had for Rick, for her kids, for family, friends, and strangers— that was healing her and putting her back together again. Love was healing her family, and her heart. Love had healed Rick.

Peg and Rick loved each other from the inside out. They endured so much together. When they were faced with infertility they were told if they made it through, they could survive anything. There were days Peg thought she would break, days she wanted to get on a plane and fly away. Dark days of fear and isolation. There are still those days, but the light is coming back; the spark is returning and the LOVE that ignited this relationship is still present. Someone called it "a different type of LOVE." But love never changes, it's the same because:

LOVE does not change.

LOVE is constant, true, and strong.

LOVE is real and authentic.

LOVE is kind and graceful.

LOVE is healing patience.

LOVE hurts and cries.

LOVE mourns.

LOVE fears.

LOVE comforts.

LOVE shines bright, always!

Chapter 18

♥

The Game Of Life

Rick learned as a child that the game of life is precious and special, something Peg learned much later in life. As Peg continued to heal her family, she realized just how precious and fragile life is. Life cannot be taken for granted. We grow from each experience, and we are responsible for our own happiness and well-being. We learn from failures, grow stronger from trauma, stay true to ourselves, and strong for others. We move forward each day with grace. There are twenty-four hours in a day and in that time, we can choose to be grateful, love deeper, and to take care of those who mean the most to us. Life can be shifted, changed, challenged, and flipped upside down, but one element can never be changed, and that is LOVE.

Rick grew up playing games. They were always a part of his life. Games brought families together, games challenged opponents, and games fostered a healthy sense of competition. Peg did not understand any of this until she met Rick and his family. When they played games there was a connection that surrounded them. The kitchen table at their home was where it all happened. A long rectangular table with oak benches. After dinner, a card game would begin. They would play for hours; laughing, talking, and challenging each other. It was where stories were told, secrets shared, and memories made. It was where they drank, laughed, and even cried. It was more than just a card game; it was a time of sharing.

Thus, as Peg healed and learned to practice self-care, Rick helped her realize that the game of life is one of patience, love, and healing. Together, they turned their "game" into a personal game of LOVE.

DATE DAY

Peg and Rick had enjoyed many games before Rick's accident. Golf, tennis, cards with friends, board games with the kids, and many more. But, as with everything else, these had to be modified after the accident. Rick and Peg modified some of their familiar favorites and found new games they could play as well. They found ways to have fun and enjoy their time together, even returning to their regular date nights that had served as such a respite when the kids were little. But now they call it, "date day!"

> *"To feel good is to feel GOD."*
> ~ **Wayne Dyer**

Mondays became Peg and Rick's favorite date day. They would go to the golf range and Rick would hit about five balls, Peg would practice, and then they would have lunch at the club. Afterwards, they looked forward to meditating, and then dinner at a place where they came to know the bartenders and bell clerks.

One particular Monday struck a chord with both of them. Their meditation instructor was a shining light. She was the voice they both needed to hear. She gave them hope and inspiration to find greatness from this trauma.

"There is a purpose, go out and find it and meditate on it. It will one day become very clear," she said to them.

They both wanted to share their story, to help others, to give back, and meditation brought that closer and clearer. Sitting in the stillness and quiet, awakening to one's soul was beginning to happen during each session. "Write that book, invent something, build that school, whatever it would be, it would be theirs! Awaken, and shine the light brighter than ever before. Whenever it begins to dim, redirect it, turn it UP! Live life with purpose." This was the message from class.

This was the message every Monday. As they both sat in stillness, the light slowly began to brighten. The more they sat in silence, the more the voice of the Universe God, or source, spoke louder.

Chapter 19

SHE SHED

Gret's Rock is small and essentially one room, an open floor plan. It offers little privacy or quiet, especially when aides, therapists, wheelchairs, etc. are in the house. Peg needed a sacred space to call her own. A place of peace, calm, and respite. This space began as a corner in the basement, but, obviously, this was not ideal. Then, one day, Peg found herself at a home goods store buying a shed. This shed was to become her sanctuary and her "She Shed."

The shed had been sitting empty since she purchased it, waiting like a friend for her to call. She started with the inside. It had to be a space of good energy. People who entered had to truly want this energy. Together, Peg and Katherine painted the inside. She and Katherine shared a special bond that was so strong.

Peg did not want perfection, as she knew all too well life was not perfect. They laughed, talked, and even cried as they painted. They told stories, and let go of the past, vowing to move forward with grace and courage. Thus, when the painting was done, love resonated inside the She Shed.

Peg refused to go to a local store and get just anything to decorate the shed. She wanted the perfect pieces with the right energy and connections for her special place. An old carpet from her sister's home that her mom helped pick out years prior. It had an energy of love. When she placed it, it immediately filled the space with warmth, as if speaking to her from a place far away. An old milk bottle from her dad. He had been working outside of Burlington twenty-five years ago and found it the day Katherine arrived home. He gave it to Peg, and it traveled with its own stories from Burlington to Williamston to Pointe Verde, landing in the perfect spot. It had been dug up with love by someone who unconditionally loved both her and her beautiful daughter. Nearby was a picture of her dad with his arms around her and her sister. She felt protected by this man whom she missed so deeply her heart hurt.

Her father's presence was real. He showed up by sending her a ladybug or a song he often would sing, especially when she needed a little more strength in her day.

Years ago, she and her mom were in an antique store on Pointe Verde and found a beautiful wicker chair. She spent a fortune on that thing! Now it was all weathered and chipped but was perfect and went right into the shed! Again, she felt a connection of love. It would be in this chair that she would begin and finish her story, her forever love story.

With these key pieces in place, the rest came together. A beautiful desk from a dear friend came from a thrift store with its own stories. A bookcase to hold books of inspiration and guidance. Big pillows made of tapestry that would serve as a meditation space. Beautiful window boxes with bright flowers were created with love. The She Shed was Peg's "safe haven" for when she needed comfort or that feeling of home she had as a little girl. She needed to feel safe within the walls of her shed, her private space of comfort.

The first time she stepped into the shed to meditate and begin a practice of self-care and change, she was terrified of what may happen. Peg knew she needed to take those first steps to begin to heal, to clear a path, to begin a journey she was ready to go on. Peg found a sense of peace and soon was crying. She was fearful, but at the same time at peace and secure in this surrounding. The space of warmth and love, with a connection to spirits she knew were always watching over her and would continue to watch over her, guiding her along this path of healing. She did not know where the path was taking her, but she knew to trust the process and go in LOVE.

HEALING SOUNDS OF NATURE

Sitting still in the She Shed, she listened, just listened. The trees swayed back and forth. The colors in the backyard were vibrant, reminding her that life would one day be vibrant for her and her family again. Bright and beautiful. Beautiful mantras chanting in the background, the birds starting to wake. It was early morning, still dark, the sun slowly coming in the windows. The bird's chirps came one at a time, as if to say, "Good morning, we are here, don't be afraid." With this sweet reassurance, Peg reminded herself not to be afraid to step out, to be free, to be me! Peg trusted Mother Earth was there at all times; protecting her, guiding her, and healing her.

With the reassurance of the sounds and rhythms of nature and her trust in Mother Earth, Peg turned her focus to the questions she had to ask herself. Questions that ultimately had to be answered for true healing to occur.

Peg knew she had to love herself in order to have enough love to put into her relationship with Rick. Even though everything had changed and flipped upside down, she was not giving up. How could she ever think of leaving her life? She trusted her heart and a process bigger than herself. She asked herself the four questions, and she added another question. "Why are you in this?" If the answer came too quickly, she would sit with it a bit. She told herself that if the answer was purely for security, that was not good enough. It was LOVE that kept her there, kept her going and moving forward.

She was preparing for the work of ultimately getting to a place of pure peace and pure love. A place to take care of Rick, their kids, and her home. Make each space safe and secure, clear everything out, and almost start again. She had no idea what was coming, but she sat with it daily and let the universe show her what to do next.

Her daily meditation practice and self-care healing would bring them to a place of peace again, she knew it in her heart. As Peg's teacher had written: "It is not despite the swamp that the lotus grows

so beautifully, it is because of the swamp it knows its magnificence."
Peg was beginning to understand how this related to her and how
the trauma she had been through was going to help her grow into
that strong, independent human she forever longed to be. She would
learn to make solid decisions and not to ask permission for anything
she chose to do. Feeling as though she would never be abandoned,
she let go knowing she could take care of herself. Trusting the changes
and the process she had to go through in order to get there.

Life had changed, and maybe, she was finally ready to accept what
was next.

Chapter 20

SECURITY

Seven sixteen was home. It was strong, it represented all that was safe. That house made her, it molded who she was. But she was always a child when she was there. Dependent on her parents, even as an adult.

Losing her dad, her hero, six years prior was completely devastating. Her dad was the first anchor in her life to die and she was torn apart. He was her constant. He enjoyed every day to the fullest. He always stayed present. He always knew what to do to calm her. "Go be with your husband and kids," he always told her. Maybe her dad was her first guru yoga teacher who led her to her yoga path?

Her dad built the house on his farm, and it was beautiful. It was built with good energy, and that is why she always felt so safe there. Even as an adult. But when her dad passed away, he took that energy with him, or maybe the energy just changed. The house became a shell. Her mother also became a shell, a woman Peg once thought was so strong was now so sad, scared, and alone. After her dad passed, whenever Peg walked into the house there was a still feeling, a heavy feeling. She would go no further than the kitchen, afraid of what she would feel and see further inside the house.

Her yoga practice and training helped her through the dark days following her dad's stroke and death, as she tried to help her mom heal. The security was gone, her dad was gone, a piece of her life was gone. The house felt empty.

Seven sixteen, where she always felt safe and secure, was being emptied out and sold. Once again Peg found herself being completely abandoned and so afraid of what lay ahead. Nothing seemed secure to her.

For six years after her dad's illness and death, Peg neglected her own healing and self-care. This was the most painful time to date in her life. It was a time of change and she fell prisoner to fear, pain, and guilt. Peg tried so hard to get her mom in a good place, but her mother's depression was too deep, and this strong woman could not be there for Peg the way she once had. The way Peg thought she always would be. Peg realized the second anchor in her life was slowly slipping away. Who was she becoming? This woman, this mother of four, grandmother of ten? She was so sad and angry. Peg tried to help her, but nothing was good enough. Their relationship changed. Peg continued to visit, but never moved past the safety of the kitchen.

MOVING THROUGH TRAUMA

When he was hit by the car, Rick became the third anchor to leave her.

Her healing began when she recognized that in order to move through this trauma she had to once again come undone, and she was not sure she was ready or could emotionally handle this again. Why relive the traumas and loss again? Wasn't it enough the first time? She thought she was supposed to let it go, not look back, and stay present. The past is done now. But she was told she needed to face it again in a way of healing, not merely surviving it.

Peg took a leap of faith and healing began. She felt the change happening. The daily practices, the meditation, and self-care she was being taught were taking her to a place of change, a place where she was able to feel safe again. Back to that feeling of being home. Peg was ready to take those memories from the house that made her and put them in her soul again. She found her safe haven. It had been the house she grew up in, but now she needed a new safe place. She needed to heal the broken part inside of her and find herself again. It would happen in time, she knew that, but she needed to commit to the practices she was being taught and do the work.

Monday night meditation was "a good one," as Rick said. Josie spoke of high vibration, loving awareness, consciousness, and digging deep within. Reminding Peg and Rick that this accident, this situation, had happened for a higher purpose, not for them to wallow in self-pity. Josie gave them a burst of energy once again. She reminded them to live with love and be positive and intentional in all of life's magic.

When Peg and Rick left the yoga studio, they both felt alive and committed to change. Peg knew what she had to do, but did Rick? Often Peg looked at him sitting on the sofa and wondered what he was thinking? She saw tears when days were tough, smiles when their kids were around. She so wanted his spirit lit up and for him to know that hope and love would get him through this. He was trying so hard.

Meanwhile, in Peg's own space of stillness, so much was being stirred up. Peg was recommitted to loving awareness, showing up, loving everyone, and seeing shifts begin to take shape. It was all going to happen. She knew this in her heart, just as she knew in her heart on January 24th, 2017, that her husband, her Rock, was not going to die. He was alive and she was alive, and life was good.

Peg's self-care practices were put into place to make her whole again, to make her strong and confident again, and to help her to manage all this. She trusted the process.

River Walk

Walking along the river, Peg looped her arm through Rick's and took a hold of his cane. She let fear go and love in, and they walked together, arm in arm, along the boardwalk. There were no words, just the sounds of nature, as soothing as music, hope, and the vibrations of the earth guiding them forward.

Peg finally let go of her fear that day; fear of falling, fear of letting him go on his own, fear of losing everything again. She now knows that nothing can stay the same, so releasing this strong emotion was a huge breakthrough she needed to overcome. Her self-care and meditation practices were showing her what the power of fear does and what path to take to clear it.

DIGGING DEEP, HOW TO HEAL

How on earth would this all work out? It was not done by forcing things to work, but rather by letting go and letting God take over. Just like she did when Rick was in the ICU. Let the faith of God and the Universe lead their path. The first step she took was to devote herself completely to self-care. To be committed to doing the work and staying in practice. To keep a toolbox of all her self-care practices, mantras, prayers, oils, etc.

Peg's self-care practice began every morning in her She Shed, her own private space. Meditation was so important in order for Peg to begin her day. Sitting silently for a half an hour or so and then reading and journaling. It set the tone for the day ahead. Quiet time was so important. She took long walks and practiced yoga every day. She surrounded their home with pictures that brought smiles to her face and objects specifically picked for that spot. She began to build tiny sacred spaces everywhere, without even realizing it. She wanted this small Pointe Verde cottage to feel warm, to feel safe, and to be filled with love.

FINDING PEACE

At first Peg thought finding peace meant no more hospital rooms and trauma units. No worries of trauma coming back. But what was this peace she was searching for? Where would it come from and how would she find it? She soon found the answer after one of her morning meditations.

Below is a quote Peg came upon when she randomly flipped through a book from her bookshelf.

"To truly find peace you must remain inactive and absolutely alert when confronted with challenging people and situations!"

~ Eckhart Tolle

The universe led Peg to the book and the exact page. Now she knew that to get to that state of peace she had to get over her own ego, fear, and insecurities. She now knew situations that occur are only energy and they can be cleared out by truly not reacting.

God and the Universe will take care of everything. God lies in us and guides us where we need to be. To find peace is to find love in everything. Love and the universe would guide Peg.

She kept trying to tell herself that *she* was going to make their life work. But in the end, she knew she had to give it to the universe, to God, and to source, knowing they would guide her in grace. In the meantime, life would unfold the way it was meant to unfold.

The day was beautiful. Peg and Rick walked the river boardwalk arm in arm, feeling whole again, feeling like the couple they needed to be to move forward. Understanding that life would not return to what it had been because they were reshaped, but also understanding what they needed to do to make this work. They had to let go of trying, let go of control, let go of "making" it work, and let it unfold the way it needed to unfold. Just trust the process. As Peg walked with Rick, she felt a strong presence guiding him and holding him.

That day on the beach, accepting this new knowledge and letting go, Peg and Rick walked in a newfound peace. "There is so much healing near the ocean!", Peg said to Rick.

"It's all about love," Rick responded.

Chapter 21

FOURTH OF JULY

Peg and Rick had taken the necessary steps to return to the ocean, the place that brought them so much happiness, hope, inner-peace, and love. At Gret's Rock they felt safe and peaceful.

There was not a cloud in the sky that day. It was July fourth weekend, and the beach would soon be packed with sunburned tourists, screaming kids, and cars bumper to bumper. Despite all of this, Rick still wanted to go. He walked out with his bathing suit and flip flops, cane in hand. "Let's go," he said. Instead of thinking just how perfect the day would be, Peg was packing the car and thinking of all the logistics involved to get Rick safely onto the beach. Where to park? Where are the bathrooms?, etc. But she agreed to go.

They immediately found the perfect parking spot. Peg unloaded everything and then, just like that, one by one, her angels appeared to help.

Peg got Rick up the stairs okay, but the beach chair fell over and a woman was right there to help her—thank GOD! Peg lathered Rick with sunscreen in a loving way. It felt good to put her hands over his naked chest. Peg read her book and Rick slept peacefully for almost two hours.

Peg tuned out the sounds around her and the only sounds she heard were the ocean waves and the wind. It was as if they were all alone on the overcrowded beach. An Irishman appeared out of nowhere and wished them well. He was so friendly, telling them all about Ireland and where he was from.

When they were ready to leave, a woman, another stranger, another angel, helped Peg pack the car and get Rick off the beach as smoothly as possible. Peg had no frustration or fear at all as she thanked this woman and thanked God for this blessing. She thanked God for the sense of relief she experienced, the sense that true healing had begun, not just physical, but emotional and spiritual healing as well. The day would forever be stamped on Peg's heart.

Peg and Rick were quiet the rest of the day, but that was okay. They were taking in what had happened, the peace of the day at the ocean. The beach left them both completely calm and content. They went to bed early that evening and slept well.

The next day they woke up feeling a little lighter and ready for a walk along the river. When they got there, Peg immediately noticed the blue sky and that once again everything was still and quiet. Rick handed her his cane, as he would do often when they tried to walk together, and she looped her arm through his. Not struggling with fear, not thinking, simply praying and walking mindfully along the path which led to a bench where they sat in total silence watching the river come alive with boats, paddle boats, and kayaks. Rick looked at Peg and said, "Come on, let's get going," and they began again!

July fourth weekend that summer came and went. The week was busy, and the kid's energy filled their home—laughter again, even a boat ride. The street was busy, and tourists crowded the beaches. When everyone was gone, the stillness came back and the silence in the house was inescapable. But instead of dreading it, Peg welcomed the stillness and silence. She was grateful, for in the silence she learned so much about herself. She went deep and listened, she found her truth, her purpose.

Rick and Peg knew to stay present in the moment and that the universe, God, and source would show them the way again. Meditation this Monday night was all about opening the Seven

Chakras, allowing energy to clear through light, letting go, releasing, and accepting. Rick had never had this experience. His third eye chakra was released, and he saw deep purple. This chakra means to open, and to follow intuition and ideas.

It was time for both of them to start living life again. Nothing was out of reach or impossible. Peg refused to allow their world to become small. Opening her heart, her mind, her body, and her spirit to all possibilities. It was all happening, and trusting the process was what they needed to do.

Revamping her home was big for Peg. She made little altars everywhere. Pictures, stones, oils, and crystals. She wanted every room to bring in LOVE and JOY. Healing candles with calming scents burned all the time and soulful music played. Colors and prints brought happiness. Her mother's vintage vase came out of storage. Everything was handpicked to raise the vibration in the house. Peg was creating a space of calmness and peace.

As the summer went on, Peg began to see glimmers of life, glimmers of times with friends again, dinners, getting dressed up and putting on makeup, good conversations and laughter. Putting her daily practices in place, meeting with her teachers, and always returning to her safe space, even if only in her mind. She was able to stay calm and steady. As her self-care practices became more of a top priority, life was coming in again for her and her family. The kids were doing well and were happy. She was able to guide them. She realized *she* was steering the ship now and accepting this meant being clear on what she wanted and needed to do. She had to put her captain hat on and take full charge of every decision and every aspect of their lives. This is something she learned from her spiritual coach.

Staying strong and present, peaceful and calm, while guiding her family and protecting them always. She was committed to this and to getting her home in order, her life in order, and moving forward with LOVE, GRACE, and FAITH!

Remember, there will always be storms in life, as well as calm seas!

Chapter 22

THE TORNADO

That morning while watching the news everything seemed fine. Then the warning came. "Seek shelter immediately!" A possible tornado had been sighted on Pointe Verde. Peg looked at Rick. A force so strong came over her and she thought, how the hell will I ever get him to the basement? Peg knew she had to get herself, Rick, and the dogs to safety. And she had to pray because we have to give our life to God, or whatever/whoever you believe in. There is a higher power taking care of us all.

The next thing Peg remembers is being huddled on the sofa in the corner of the basement with Rick and their dogs. She closed her eyes and prayed. She did not stop until the sounds of the tornado passing through stopped.

They managed to get back upstairs with help from Rick's nephew, another angel sent by God to help them. Power was lost, but there was no damage to their small home.

This was all another reminder of how fragile life was, and how in a blink everything can change. And a reminder to find joy in each moment, to find laughter, to dance, to listen to music, to be silly, and not to take things too seriously. Always say I love you. We never know when that storm will hit, when the time will come to face destruction and chaos in our lives.

Rick's energy in that basement was so strong Peg felt safe and not at all alone. Even though physically he struggled, spiritually he was present. He was strong and calm.

They were together, protecting each other. While the storm raged, they played a game by candlelight. The storm passed and neither of them thought of the next day. They were present in the moment.

After the storm, Peg revisited the tragedy, the trauma, accidents, and deaths and remembered…"THE SUN ALWAYS RISES."

THE NEXT DAY

Peg and Rick walked slowly out to the ocean on a stretch of boardwalk. The sun was setting, giving them time to make it to the end. This was the most beautiful spot on Pointe Verde. Step by step, they took everything in—the smells of the ocean and marsh, the sounds of the seagulls, the taste of the salt water in the air, the touch of each other's hands. It took 600 steps to be exact, and one hour. The sandbar was spectacular!

They met a friend with her two children along the way. The children reminded them of Katherine and Peter at ages ten and twelve, some of their best times on the beaches of Pointe Verde. Peg recalled how their smiles lit up her world. She told her friend, "Make a memory of this time, it goes so fast!"

Continuing onward in silence, they made it to the end of the boardwalk. They sat together and were completely alone. But God was with them, Peg felt His presence.

"Look at this view, Rick! Isn't it amazing?"

Rick pulled her close to his heart, wrapped his strong arms around her, and said, "Ya, it's amazing!"

LIVING **LOVE**

Josie told Peg to get Rick's feet in the sand. "Go outside, BREATHE THE AIR OR HUG A TREE!" Peg was pretty sure Josie meant there at the beach, but she felt ready to take on an adventure. Her first with Rick since his hip surgery. "Surprise!" She called Josie from their hotel room in Cancun—yes Cancun! Peg was in tears, but she was pretty sure she was just as surprised as Josie at where they were! Peg called desperately seeking Josie's help and support as Rick was so ill!!

When Sara first asked Peg and Rick to go to Mexico, Peg simply froze. All her old feelings of fear ran through her physical body. Her breath quickened, her arms became numb, and her heart raced. How in the world would she get him there? How would this work, what if something happened? She took a leap of faith, called Rick, and asked him what he thought. "Let's go! I am retired now!" he said.

Peg, in this absolutely beautiful place, crying because she now realized how vacations would look for them from now on. The reality hit her full in the face. Do I want to be pushing Rick around in a wheelchair in this resort she thought to herself? NO!! She wanted to go for walks at sunset. She wanted to go to the gym together, sit by the pool and meet people, drink margaritas, and laugh. But none of that was happening and she felt depleted. "Was all her work for nothing? Are we going to make it?" she said out loud. Jesus, her mind was flooding at that moment.

The safety of home protected them from the reality of Rick's TBI, and all the challenges they had to face. Being in this resort magnified all the challenges.

Peg called on her spiritual adviser who immediately told Peg to remember everything. Remember your practices, take care of yourself so you are able to care for Rick during this fragile time. Try to remember all of this. Peg pulled the covers over her head and fell into a deep sleep. She covered herself tightly in the blanket, seeking as much comfort as possible. She closed her eyes and slept it off like a hangover.

Their room overlooked the ocean, and it was magnificent. No doubt the change of scenery was good for both of them. But Peg needed to find a silver lining in this trip. The day before they literally sat in the room all day. Rick had a bad day and Peg went into a dark hole. "It's okay not to be okay," Peg thought, but she soon remembered to raise her vibration and continue on. Rick and I are a force, and we will get through this, she told herself.

The trip to Mexico was a breakthrough for both of them. They needed to prove to themselves that they could travel again. And they had to accept the challenges that came along with it. They were able to determine what they could do, and what they were willing to never do again. Accepting this was hard. But if they were going to love their life again, there were things that might be uncomfortable that they would have to overcome, or simply avoid ever doing again.

LEAVING FOR FLORIDA

The snow was falling that morning on Pointe Verde. It was cold, so cold, the wind blowing hard. They made the decision to leave the cold winters and spend this time in the warmth of the Florida sunshine. It was so much better for Rick's continued healing. Peg put on her rain boots, her down jacket, hat, scarf, and gloves and ventured to the coffee shop to stock up on her favorite coffee. She walked in, said hello to the owner, got her coffee, and sat for a moment in silence. She took in the comfortable feeling she so loved about this spot. It's where she hung out with her favorite people, and she loved the coffee. She looked around and saw the enormous Christmas tree in the center of the shop and smiled.

She knew then why she went there! Her self-care practice had kicked in without her even knowing it. She knew what she needed that day to fill her cup. It was the coffee she loved, a hug from a friend, and the safe comfortable feeling of that shop. She had stopped everything and done this for herself.

She had lost herself, forgotten what brought her joy and comfort, but now she was tending to her own needs and wants foremost. When you are a caregiver, your life simply stops, no matter what anyone says. You become completely engrossed in the well-being of your loved one.

At first, she had been in survival mode, treading water to make sure her family was okay. Making sure her husband was cared for and their kids were okay. Making sure their household was being run properly. Dealing with lawyers, insurance people, hospitals, doctors, therapists, aides, and just the day-to-day functions of a home. She was doing absolutely everything. Paying all the bills, dealing with all the finances, everything right down to taking the garbage out and picking up the dog poop! It was like she was on autopilot and all of a sudden, she CRASHED!

Peg got off the plane in Florida and felt lost! They were now in a strange house with nothing of their own, no friends around, and no real community. Peg froze, trying to breathe deep. They were renting a home in Florida for the winter. Once again, they were getting a home ready (this time in Florida) so Rick would be safe and comfortable. In the meantime, they were staying in a rental.

But it was the beginning of Peg's own journey home, to herself, her truth, and her spirit. So she called on the universe and God to show her the way. She let go and trusted this was where they were supposed to be.

The first thing she did was to light a candle and buy some beautiful flowers. She sat quietly in meditation and began to feel at peace.

Chapter 23

COURAGE

Thinking we would be back home by spring, we had only secured our rental through March. But Covid had other plans, and we found ourselves scrambling for a place to live during lockdown in FL. Thus, we moved for a third time this year with four dishes, four forks, four knives, four spoons, and a pot. No sheets, no towels, at the bare minimum it was a tear down house offered at a cheap rent for the month of April. We walked into a home decorated like the Addams Family house. Dusty and grim—brown and black dreary furnishings, fake plants everywhere, wall to wall beige carpeting. A musky smell. It was horrible, and I felt like the rug was literally pulled from under me.

I found myself longing for the comforts of my own home. I wanted to be close to those I loved and cared for even though we could not see each other. It was so scary; I will not lie. I felt like I needed to cry, and yes, I was scared.

What to do—curl up like a ball and stop? NOPE! Again, sitting with the hurt, the pain, the fear, and all of it, letting it stew and come up as it would. And then becoming an observer as I had been taught. I knew I had to figure out how I wanted this to look so that it would feel right and safe.

We were lying in bed, and I told Rick I felt like everything had been taken, our home, our things, our life as we knew it—I felt like an empty shell and was scared to death. The weeks in the dark house in Florida went by very slowly.

I got up and meditated on all of this. In doing so, I remembered that I had NOT lost LOVE. LOVE for my kids and husband, family and friends, and my world. With my possessions gone and my home gone, I still had the family I will protect till the end.

When we sit with our worries and allow them to surface, we can tend to them, and to ourselves, and move through the storm with grace, love, and hope.

When we initially moved to Gret's Rock, I felt unable to make that home permanent. Something was holding me back and I could not put my finger on it. But being away, I realized how home felt and I could not wait to get back and dive into that space, making it absolutely home! Warm and comforting, inviting in every way.

What does JOY mean…??

HOME!!

As we pulled into Gret's Rock my entire body felt warm. I felt safe and secure and finally able to let out the breath I had been holding in for the past month. Suddenly, this space felt like HOME! For the past three years I was just existing here, trying to make it through each day, putting on a front that this was HOME, when all along something was missing and I could not figure out what. As I walked in the door, my heart was full and I realized what had been missing here was ME! My true authentic self had never been fully present in this space. Since we moved here from Williamston, I was not present for anything that brought me joy. The heartbeat of my home was missing. I was missing.

Quickly, I realized this is where we were supposed to be. This is where the healing would truly begin. Staying the course and embracing everything. Love is the center of everything. This small home would bring us much JOY. I am present to everything I do in it. Cleaning, decorating, cooking, and just bringing in energy, good energy to make everything whole and complete again.

In times of crisis, we need to return to the trauma, sit with it, let it stew and bubble up. Then we are ready, move forward, move through it. Finding the tools to help us is the key. Finding the things that bring JOY—not just happiness, but JOY. The things that make us shiver and bubble inside, the things which can calm us. For me, I know it has always been my husband and my kids. Now the structure we live in is called HOME!

SETTLED IN

Here I am in our beautiful new home in Florida. After having felt displaced, we have a space to call home. Florida will never hold the memories we built at Gret's Rock, but it is a place where Rick will feel comfortable as life goes on and he continues to heal. We are blessed that he can escape the cold winters and be able to get out in the warmth. We are both grateful for our life and how far we have come. It has been so difficult, and we have walked and continue to walk through flames and challenges. Rick is more independent now and we are content with our quiet days of reading, watching shows, cooking dinner, and just being.

The first time I dropped Rick off with his trainer was when I realized how our life would be. I was overwhelmed with how far he had come. Walking one step at a time with his cane, using his full concentration not to fall. I stayed in the car and watched as my heart began to break from seeing my strong, beautiful husband and this life he now has to work through. The future was unknown.

As I watched, I called on the Archangel Michael to walk beside him, I took a deep breath and drove away with tears running down my face.

This is a reminder that in order to heal you have to stay in the fire and face the trauma head on. Stay with the uncomfortable feelings and don't run away. Don't stay busy or try to numb the pain. Be with it, cry, and scream, but move on with grace. Truly, what else could I have done?

As I sat in the coffee shop with Kai, my friend who truly helped me make our villa into a home and helped make certain every detail was in place for us, I found the strength to move forward. She encouraged me to let go of self-doubt and fear. Our home is complete and our life as we now know it is real. It's here. Our villa has been transformed into our home. As time went by, I found my true north. My true self from the inside. My spirit has been lit again. After four long years, I feel life, strength, and joy coming back, one day at a time.

Chapter 24

THE WORLD HAS STOPPED

I find myself without words, trying to wrap my head around yet another life changing event. An event so big it is changing our culture, our world, our planet, our people, our friends, our families, our homes, and communities. I sit here and continue on as if nothing has happened, but in this part of my story I have to STOP, like everyone else. I need to reflect on what is going on and hopefully use my practices to get through a time so unreal.

The Covid-19 virus has hit America and the world. I find myself in self-isolation along with everyone else, talking with friends and family via Zoom calls and FaceTime. Wishing so much to touch again, to hug family, to see my son and daughter. It's such an odd time.

My life in the past few years has felt no different, honestly. Rick and I have been isolated from so much of the world around us. Our days are very scheduled and do not involve getting out much. Socializing with friends and family has been limited, slowly getting back but very limited. We were not able to travel, and Rick was certainly not able to get out alone. Hours turned into days which turned into months which turned into years of hoping things would change, hoping for freedom again. We take so much for granted. The mere act of jumping into a car and going to see a friend or going to the store has ended for a while. This reality hit both Rick and me hard. This is what life was like for us in so many ways the past three years and will be long after this time is over. When the world stops and you are forced to shut down, how do you cope—by simply being GRATEFUL!

Being grateful for your health

Being grateful for your family and those you love

Being grateful for your friends and communities

Being grateful for sunshine

Being grateful for nature

Being grateful for food and essential goods

Being grateful for music

Being grateful for literature

Being grateful for movies, TV shows, and Netflix

Being grateful for the internet to connect with others

Being grateful for warmth

Being grateful for heat

Being grateful for jobs and a home

Being grateful for freedom

Being grateful for life

When you are "stuck" inside, you are almost forced to find glory in the smallest ways of being. Close your eyes and reflect....reflect on the beauty of life, the grace of God, and the magnificence of this universe. It's a gift—these are gifts which I guarantee you will never take for granted again.

Always end your conversations with, "I love you." You do not know what tomorrow will bring.

Be safe, my friends.

I love you,
Margaret

As I look back at this story, my story, our story, I see how this life could seem privileged, but I prefer to call it blessed. I was blessed with a beautiful life. A husband strong and loving in every way, two children who continue to stay by my side and have my back, friends and family, a beautiful home, and good health. We had it all and never took one of these blessings for granted.

My life was flipped. Memories of all the events I talk about in this book have been wiped from Rick's mind. Our page at this point is blank as we try to build new memories with the little we can share together.

Sure, we fought, and we had our share of struggles, but I choose not to share that part of my life because none of that matters. Especially when I see what our true struggles have been over the past five years and will continue to be for the rest of our lives. I choose to talk about all the positive and good blessings in my life. I will continue to rewrite our love story, here in the comfort of our home, Gret's Rock.

Acknowledgments

To my husband, Rick, my best friend. The true "Rock" of our family whose strength continues to amaze me everyday.

To my amazing son and daughter. You have been by my side through it all. We cried and we laughed. We have been through the dark days together. You pulled me up and helped me move on. I adore you.

To my beautiful sister Pauline, your strength, love, and support for my family has been amazing. You are truly an anchor in my life.

To all my family and friends (you know who you are) who helped my family, and helped me get through the tough days. You stepped up without even realizing how much you meant to me. I love you.

To my dear friend Chris, who has always been there for me. I will be forever grateful for our early morning conversations each day.

To my soul sister, Tammey, I will forever treasure our sunsets together.

To my "Tribe Inside" self-healers group led by my trauma and spiritual coach, Sarah. You allowed me to come apart and held me in the space we share together. Sarah led me through self-care practices and gave me the tools I needed to slowly heal from the inside. Without this group of women, I never would never have found my voice and my truth. You are forever in my heart. Peace always, to each of you.

To my therapist, who I continue to work with. Finding the strength to see a therapist and trust that person was so scary, but I did and will be forever grateful for his help and care.

To Kristen and Miara from PRESStinely. Thank you for helping me and guiding me, and all your patience in getting Gret's Rock published.

To my editor, Kristin Davis. I thank you for organizing, editing, and helping me with the flow of my story.

To every person (Angels) I have met along this journey who held me in a space of care and LOVE.

Made in United States
North Haven, CT
04 December 2022

27801027R00072